THE PHOENIX NEST

Margaret Hermes

Contemporary Books, Inc.
Chicago

Library of Congress Cataloging in Publication Data

Hermes, Margaret.
    The phoenix nest.

    I. Title.
PS3558.E686P47   1981   813'.54   80-70641
ISBN 0-8092-5905-2   AACR2

Copyright © 1981 by Margaret Hermes
All rights reserved
Published by Contemporary Books, Inc.
180 North Michigan Avenue, Chicago, Illinois 60601
Manufactured in the United States of America
Library of Congress Catalog Card Number: 80-70641
International Standard Book Number: 0-8092-5905-2

Published simultaneously in Canada by
Beaverbooks, Ltd.
150 Lesmill Road
Don Mills, Ontario M3B 2T5
Canada

For CHRIS LANGE and for PETER

Beauty, truth, and rarity
Grace in all simplicity,
Here enclos'd in cinders lie.

Death is now the phoenix' nest . . .

from *The Phoenix and the Turtle*
William Shakespeare

THE
PHOENIX
NEST

CHAPTER 1

She nearly lost her footing on the ridge. A great shudder passed over her body, and as she extended her foot to balance herself she attempted to parallel that maneuver in her thoughts. "The police. Now I must go to the police." She stepped back, gingerly avoiding any damage to her hose from the coarse brush that clung arduously to the overhang. Quickly, now that it was time to act, she made her way back to her car. She drove directly to the sheriff's office and asked to speak to whomever was in charge.

"About what, lady?" the long young man with the apricot-sized Adam's apple mumbled into the pages of Chandler's *Lady in the Lake*. Then, glancing up and taking in her appearance, he sat up in his chair, called her ma'am and passed her along to Trout.

Trout sat across the desk from her and made his own tally. An attractive woman, mid-thirties he guessed, elegantly dressed in the middle of the day. She wore grey—suit, shoes, purse, even a hat. He was not an insensitive man, but women's fashion was a subject that failed to intrigue him. Still, he felt that this woman's appearance placed her in some bygone era. His eyes dropped to her hands and his appreciation of consistency was rewarded—she held a pair of grey leather gloves. It wasn't that she looked out of date—classic, that was it. Grace Kelly playing the role of the English aristocrat's lady. Composed but anxious. Distant but almost palpably feminine. This impression was still forming when, "Are you an actress?" Trout asked suddenly.

"No," startled.

"Forgive me. Is there something with which I can help you?"

"No. Rather, I'm here to report . . . I just witnessed a suicide."

"Who . . . ?"

"I don't know. I have no idea."

"The body?"

"Gone. I did look."

"Perhaps you had better tell me what you can, and I'll spare us both these staccato interruptions." He tore off the top sheet on the pad in front of him and poised his pen above the paper. "Go ahead. Wait, would you care for something—coffee, water? Give you a chance to collect your thoughts."

"A cigarette, please, if you have one."

She drew one out of the pack he extended, then waited for him to light it. It flashed through his mind that there was indeed something sensual about lighting a cigarette for a woman. He was not pleased with the reflection. He did not like the image of men as protectors/toadies. And he did not like the feelings of manliness she was stirring in him, a sort of hearts-and-flowers romantic urge to impress her. He caught himself hoping for the opportunity to perform mental gymnastics in her presence, the way he might have done handsprings had their paths crossed thirty years ago. Well, that was his own personal toothache and he would probe it cautiously later, worrying at it with his mind's tongue until he determined whether it was just a passing twinge or something requiring attention and repair.

"I was driving along the ocean road about twelve or fifteen miles from here. As I pulled around a large bend, I came upon a sort of scenic overlook. There was a car parked close to the rim. I particularly noticed it as it was in a head-on position, the front end just inches from the edge. Then I saw the man standing there in front of the car. My attention went back to the road briefly—I was just pulling out of the curve. I looked in my rearview mirror. The man was gone. I think I was confused. I drove on a bit farther when I realized the significance of what I had just seen or, rather, didn't see. I came to a gravel road that led down to an abandoned cannery, turned the car around and drove back to the overlook. When I got out of my car I looked around and looked into the man's car. There was nothing. No one. And no place to go except straight down. I knew I would have seen the man if he were still in the vicinity—it's just sheer slopes and open spaces—so I looked down into the water. I saw nothing there, either, but the drop must be at least two hundred feet. Then I came to you." This last was said simply and with the air of a peer of the realm discharging a distasteful duty, turning an awkward matter over to the competent if pedestrian care of the local constable.

Peer of the realm, thought Trout, in a coastal town in Maine. I've got to stop gawking at the titles on the paperback rack when I'm standing in checkout lines. Next I'll envision her living in some remote mansion surrounded by heather and sinister forces.

He cleared his throat and his mind simultaneously. "Would you recognize this man if you were to see him again?"

"I only saw him briefly, but, yes, I think I would recognize the body." Trout noted the correction. "Possibly the best means of ascertaining his identity would be to determine the ownership of the car. It was a dark green Audi. I don't know what year. I copied down the license number and removed the keys from the ignition. I wasn't sure if I should tamper with the car, but I thought it would interfere more with an investigation if the car were stolen." She opened her purse and took out a small folded piece of paper and a ring of keys and placed them on the corner of the desk. "I was, of course, mindful of not removing my gloves."

Trout called Agronski into his office and, sliding the paper across to him, instructed him to trace the license number. "I wish all our witnesses might be as clearheaded, Mrs. . . . apparently I could take a leaf from your book. I'm afraid I didn't even ask your name."

"Miss Galatea. Eve Galatea."

Not married and not Ms. Why do I feel that the latter half of the twentieth century has passed her by? Trout leaned forward "Address, please?"

"404 Merriweather, Boston. I have been driving through Maine doing some sketching along the way."

"Ah, you are an artist."

"If you mean that I support myself by my drawings, no. I am one of those fortunate people with an income. The money is there; my work is in determining how to spend it. This is really a vacation."

"After Agronski runs the plate number through I'd like you to accompany me back to the overlook. You think you are up to it?"

"If you believe it's necessary," Eve Galatea spread her hands in a gesture of resignation. "I should like to have that cup of coffee now, if I may."

"Certainly. Cuppa reggaler? My erudition surprises you? I went to school in Bahston. Native son makes good in the outside world and makes up for it by returning to his rightful place. Ayuh." Trout stuck his head outside the door. "Homer, coffee for Miss Galatea, with cream."

Amusement tugged at the corners of her eyes. "A Mainer who speaks Bostonese with the midwestern flatness of a network newscaster."

"That took cultivation. I discovered at school that it was anathema to be from the Midwest and even worse to sound as though you were from anywhere else." Homer brought the coffee in, turned on his heels and was out of the room in one motion. Too young to appreciate anything not overexposed or in first bloom, thought Trout, looking after him and sighing.

"It's entirely unconscious now, my accent or lack of it," he resumed. "I find yours difficult to place. You don't drop your Rs and tack them onto stray vowels. Am I correct in presuming you are not Boston born and bred?"

"Your experience of Bostonians must have been fairly limited, but, yes, I've lived in many places. My diction is the mongrel offspring of a transient way of life," she said with gentle self-mockery. "I have a chameleon's tongue. Given enough time in your fair village I would likely acquire the soothing custom of placing a period after each word uttered."

Trout felt something kindle in him, sparked by her voice. It was warm and deep and, like everything else about her, very controlled. "I cannot imagine your being at the mercy of even your own subconscious, let alone dictated to by your environment. If you were to speak with a brogue after twenty years' residence in Dublin it would be because on the three hundred and sixty-fourth day of the nineteenth year you had decided to do so."

Miss Galatea looked at him sharply, as though searching for some insult behind his words and, finding none, relaxed and smiled vaguely. "You see me as the victim of feminine caprice, then. My choices dictated by whim."

"On the contrary, I find you exceedingly feminine but not the least bit whimsical." The hard look came into her eyes again. "I'm sorry if I've offended you. Yes, Agronski, what have you got?"

The man stood in the doorway, his body stiff, but interrupting with his eyes. "The car," he said in obvious agitation. "Christ, sir, you're not going to believe this." Agronski had the annoying habit of calling Trout "sir" while on duty. Trout had tried to ease him out of it with no success. It made Trout feel as though he *ought* to patronize him, inquire after his wife, send christening gifts and make periodic paternal speeches.

"I'd welcome that chance," said Trout with harnessed impatience.

"It's registered to Nathan Adams. The same vehicle that

disappeared when he did his vanishing act fourteen months ago."

Trout let out a hiss of air as though Agronski's announcement had caught him in the solar plexus. "Curiouser and curiouser. All right Agronski, take the patrol car up to the overlook, rope off the area and keep the tourists from tramping through to admire the view. Miss Galatea, please try to make yourself comfortable in the outer room. I have some phoning to do. State and federal brass are going to want to go over the area and our findings with everything from a pitchfork to the proverbial fine-toothed comb. And, Agronski, spill this juice to anyone and I'll have your head. We'll have the press all over us soon enough. Right now we just don't have the manpower to keep the muckrakers from plowing under evidence."

Agronski nodded with a hurt look clouding his normally sunny brow and took his departure. Eve Galatea shot a questioning look at Trout. which he ignored. As she gathered up her belongings, Trout called, "Homer, get the state's attorney general on the line and don't trot in here looking bewildered. Just do it or you'll be back bagging groceries at the IGA." Trout bent over his desk, making rapid notes on a fresh sheet of yellow legal paper. As the light on his desk phone glowed he glanced up. Reaching for the receiver, he barely had time to blink in astonishment. My God, with those heels on, the woman must be nearly six feet tall. Then, "Hello, sir. Trout, Halesport County Sheriff. We have begun investigation of a possible suicide that I think will very much interest you . . ."

Trout was not pondering the disappearance of Nathan Adams, or whether this suicide would lay to rest the question of his whereabouts, or what the net effect of the investigation would be on his own career. He deliberately chose not to dwell on the disturbing proximity of the woman seated beside him but to concentrate on his car. Driving was possibly the only activity that offered him total relaxation. Certainly better than dream-diluted sleep. Past and future were irrelevant. His body became a mass of instinct, turning with the wheels, flowing with the curves.

The county could afford to purchase and support only one patrol car. When he took the job eleven years ago, Trout was given the option of having that for his private use or of buying the vehicle of his choice out of pocket and receiving a maintenance subsidy. He chose the latter. Smiling to himself, he recalled the local grumbling when about four years ago he and his wife Enid solemnly decided that her Volkswagen must be junked. It had served them faithfully since before their marriage, but even affection and loyalty toward their old bug had finally, in tandem with the car, run itself into the ground. Besides, it was entirely impractical now with Enid's dabbling in local antiques turning into her major occupation and providing, on an irregular basis, half their income. So she inherited his station wagon, and he went on the prowl for another large, comfortable, conservative car suitable for his position and for transporting his daughter's soccer team and gardening supplies. He liked gardening. It came close to driving in the tranquility it provided.

He was as surprised as the people of Fells Harbor with his choice of a used and bruised Alfa Romeo, which he had had lovingly mended and refurbished by Ellswood Howett. Howett ran a local service station and didn't get much opportunity to practice his gift of restoring cars, so he was grateful to Trout for what he considered his masterpiece and defended him staunchly to the natives who opined that a foreign sports car was the initial and irrefutable evidence of corruption and degeneracy. Only Enid had reacted with amusement, saying that she thought his masculine ego had greyed at least ten years prematurely. In the intervening years Trout showed no further signs of moral decay and the town's outrage diminished to periodic sighs and head-shakings.

Trout still understood little of the workings of the car and relied on Howett to keep their love child healthy, but driving it was his foremost pleasure. He took physical comfort in his proximity to the road. And what a magnificent road the coast drive was—the end product of a WPA and Civilian Conservation Corps collaboration during the thirties. It had no formal title, just Highway 41, but it had long been a source of pride among the coastal towns. It was a sculpture chiseled from the cliffs with the resulting rock debris set in concrete to form irregular walls guarding the more treacherous curves.

"Who is Nathan Adams?"

Trout turned to his passenger, the abrupt question invading his careful detachment. Trout was annoyed with himself as he became conscious of his acute awareness of her. Even while he had been thinking of his car, his mechanic, and his wife, he had noted the position of her hands as they lay in her lap, the angle of her head as she watched the flitting scenery, the rise and fall of her breathing.

"Head of the Hornsby brokerage firm. Inherited his position. His mother was Hornsby. Still is, for that matter. His father took over the firm while Gerald Hornsby was still alive. Main office in New York. Primary residence there, too, but the Hornsby family has always maintained a 'cottage' here. Very impressive place. Beautifully appointed, as my Aunt Agatha would say."

"You're well acquainted with the family, I take it?"

"Hardly, My initial view of the interior was by way of the silver screen."

"Pardon?"

"The family fortune has dwindled drastically so a few years ago they consented to having the house and estate used as the setting in the filming of *The Portrait of a Lady*."

"The Henry James novel."

"Yes. Did you see the movie?"

"No."

"Pity. A financial disaster. For everyone but Nathan Adams. The fee for the use of the premises did not depend upon the box office returns, naturally." Trout sighed, "I thought it was an exceptionally fine film, but it was doomed, of course. The only naked limbs to be seen were those of the antique furniture. If only some of the details had been modernized in the screenplay—say, making the old man's death a result of slow poisoning by his wife who for years had been maintaining a lesbian liaison with Madame Merle. Now that would have had them standing in line. Probably had its longest run locally to satisfy curiosity about how the resident nobility lives and to indulge fond relatives who came to view and review the few natives who copped parts as extras."

He glanced up from the road to find Eve Galatea's eyes hard upon him. He felt suddenly embarrassed. Foolish, he thought; I've said nothing so very personal. Nevertheless his tone was crisply professional as he hurried on. "The money from the film company was far short of what was required to replenish the family coffers. Adams righted that by careful but extensive embezzlement from the brokerage firm, which was discovered about a year ago after his disappearance. You probably read about it at the time."

"Yes, I think perhaps I did. Has the money been recovered?"

"No. Adams had been vacationing here. Since his point of departure was in our jurisdiction, we were involved in the search and, as they say, he and the funds disappeared without a trace."

"Until today."

"Maybe." Trout pulled the Alfa Romeo over to the edge of the parking area. "Well, Agronski, what is it?"

Indeed, it did not take a detective to deduce that the man had something to impart. His eyes were dancing with excitement even if he managed, with no mean effort, to keep his feet from following suit. "An envelope, sir. On the dashboard. Addressed to Mrs. Mildred Hornsby Adams." This oral telegram elicited a grunt from Trout. He drew the keys to the Audi from his pocket, unlocked the car and gingerly removed the envelope with his handkerchief.

"You have gloves and dusting kit?"

"Right here."

"Then you do the honors."

Agronski hummed happily at his task. "A couple of clear prints on the envelope, sir. Shall I remove the contents?"

And there it was. Most tidy. First a confession as to past misdeeds, then expressions of remorse at tarnishing the family's glossy name, then a statement of intention, and finally an avowal of filial love, complimentary close, Nathan.

"Just about makes the lab work a formality," murmured Agronski, his disappointment coloring his voice. Opportunities for honing his skills were rare and treasured.

"Could be forged," said Trout in condolence.

"Handwriting analysis will probably show otherwise," mourned Agronski. "What would the purpose be?"

"None. Miss Galatea's assessment was correct. He couldn't have disappeared anywhere but down in the time it took her to swing back here, and the only way down . . . Well, it's the perfect spot for it; not much chance of bungling the job."

"And it's not the sort of thing one man would willingly do for another, except at gunpoint. Are you sure the man you saw was alone, ma'am?"

"Quite."

"Well, sir, it could hardly be a ruse to end the investigation under the circumstances."

"No." Trout was suddenly angry, though the cause of his belligerence was unclear even to him. "Emily Post's book of etiquette must have a section on the proper form a suicide note should take. Or maybe it's one of those fine points acquired at prep school." Agronski watched him curiously as he covered the area with Eve Galatea, eliciting a repetition of what she had seen and where.

There was no sign of the body on the rocks or in the water below. The likelihood of the corpse ever being recovered was slim. The currents were strong here and if the body hadn't already been carried out to sea there were so many underwater caverns and rock formations that it would probaby remain in the brackish water, eternally dancing with the waves, eyes glaring, hair billowing. I wonder, thought Trout, how long it takes a body to decompose in the sea. Does the salt act as a preservative or does it eat away at the flesh? He shut his eyes tight to rid himself of the vision.

"I don't think there is anything more you can help us with here, Miss Galatea. I'll take you back to the station now, if you don't mind. We want to determine if you can pick out Adams' face, but with no police record prior to his disappearance there's no mug shot. Since we've only a shapshot of him on file, Homer had to round up some other photos to test your recognition of the man you saw on the cliff. He should have assembled quite a collection by now."

CHAPTER 2

Once more Trout was taking the turns on the coast road and on this occasion his thoughts were darting and weaving as well. Eve Galatea had had no trouble identifying the photograph of Nathan Adams. She had skimmed through the pictures rather quickly, spreading them out on his desk with one hand in the manner of a dealer fanning the cards. She selected Adams' picture without hesitation. Yes, she said, she had seen him only briefly, but her view of him was unobstructed and the bizarre nature of the circumstances had served to freeze his image on her brain.

Trout smiled to himself, speculating on Homer's tribulations as he scurried around town begging pictures of the menfolk, "To be returned, ma'am; I'll see to it myself." There was no one lower on the totem pole to see to it, anyway. Despite Homer's desire to dazzle in his virginal career as a law enforcement officer, he was a surprisingly efficient and uncomplaining kid. The bluster would wear off, Trout considered, when

Homer stopped dreaming that in a year or so, after he had proven himself superior to his superiors, he would be offered the position of Bangor chief of police or, at the very least, Trout's own job. He'll stop dreaming, mused Trout, and he'll be one of the lucky ones. He'll mislay his dream. He won't have to give it up; he'll just forget it had ever existed.

Trout was en route to the Hornsby house. Mildred Hornsby Adams had to be told. Trout had never met the lady, even while making inquiries into her son's sudden departure. When the scandal first broke, the family had retired to New York to lick its wounds and clothe itself in the anonymity of the city. This summer, though, it was business as usual, which is to say virtually no business at all in the months of June through August. It was like stepping backwards into another era. When even the wealthiest of families were finding it impossible to hang on to their "country" estates, to keep the staff these palaces required, simply to maintain the grounds—when one by one they were deeded to historic preservation societies which conducted paying tours and leased the premises to charity fund raisers—Mrs. Mildred Hornsby Adams, her two sons, and a melange of guests summered annually at their "place" on Fells Harbor.

Even though his sensibilities shrank from the ordeal of having to burden this woman with the suicide of her younger son, Trout was aware of a rising curiosity at the prospect of meeting her. She must be in her late seventies now. He recalled hearing that she had married late, around thirty-five or so, and then only after having proposed to Adams herself. The scandalous act was supposed to have taken place here in Fells Harbor. The story went that Adams had come to pay court to Gerald Hornsby and finding that the father was not much impressed by his business acumen or his puckish smile, he accepted the courtship of the only living heir. It still amused Trout to speculate on how that bit of gossip was first bandied about. His Aunt Agatha, who had been married and widowed twice, announced stentorially at an odd moment that, unlike *some* people, she at least had never found it necessary to purchase a

husband, thankyouverymuch. How his Aunt Agatha or any of
the local people should acquire such detailed knowledge of the
intimate dealings of the Hornsby house defied his comprehen-
sion. He doubted the authenticity of the marriage tale but knew
he would secretly be disappointed if it were proved false. The
Hornsby mythology served to make Mildred Hornsby Adams
more intriguing and was, along with the craggy coastline, one
of the chief local delights.

As he rang the bell of the Hornsby house, Trout struggled
between professional detachment and repugnance at his task.
He speculated on the role of the young woman who piloted him
into the drawing room. Maid? Not dressed for it. Housekeeper?
Not enough authority in her manner. Besides, all housekeepers
are perpetually middle-aged. Certainly not a relative or a
guest. She would have introduced herself, at least shown some
curiosity instead of merely nodding deferentially. Secretary?
That's it. Accustomed to carrying messages and unaccustomed
to being looked at.

When he had settled that question to his satisfaction, Trout
took in the decor of the room itself. It was fitted out with
damask draperies and rose velvet cushions, giving it a deter-
minedly Victorian air. He further postponed anticipating the
delivery of his message by wondering why such rooms in such
houses were called "drawing" rooms. Someone sometime must
have had a reason for the appellation. He ruled out the skill of
drawing as having any connection. Perhaps in a different age
people were drawn to the rooms by the entertainments offered
therein. Or something as simple as being the first room in
which the draperies were drawn daily. Trout was in the midst
of these unrewarding musings when he realized that Gerald
Adams was staring at him, framed in the doorway, a picture of
indecision.

Trout had seen this other Adams a number of times over the
years, though they had never spoken. He was again startled at
the lack of resemblance to his brother. Gerald Adams was a
very large man, burly and quite tall. Born almost ten years
before his younger brother, he had the appearance and the

opportunity to become a likely wielder of power. But apparently all such inclination had been inherited by the younger, the almost delicate Nathan. Jacob and Esau flashed through Trout's head.

Having arrived at the decision to enter the room, Gerald Adams stepped forward and announced, "My mother will be down shortly." Taking that as instruction to state his business quickly and be gone before his presence was made known to and disturbed the old woman, Trout was slightly annoyed when he realized that Adams was not donning the man-of-the-family role but rather suggesting that he take up the reason for his call with the grande dame herself.

"I think, Mr. Adams, it might be better if we spoke first. Your mother should receive this news from a family member." Gerald Adams looked as though he were about to spring from the room, so Trout added firmly, "It's about your brother."

"You've caught Nathan, then?" Gerald's eyes darted about as though expecting his brother to pop up from behind the settee or around the secretary bookcase. Trout gave up all thoughts of softening the blow. He just wanted to deliver his announcement before the man refused to hear more and left him to face the mother alone.

"We have good reason to believe he took his own life today by leaping from the overlook near the big bend on the coast road. There is a corroborating witness and this." He handed over a photocopy of the suicide letter. "It was left in his car."

Gerald glanced at the paper. "Nathan always was thorough. We were too far apart in . . . age to be playmates, but I used to watch him. He'd say when he was just a kid that if he ever chose to kill himself, it would be by driving off that cliff. He'd say that when we were in the car, passing the spot, and I always believed him. Odd that he jumped, though. But, then, he was remarkably adaptable—not that he'd ever settle for less than he wanted—but he was capable of lying in wait for the perfect moment. I admired that.

"My sophomore year in college I was facing expulsion—a fraternity party and a stupid drunken prank that ended in a student's death, but no formal charges against any of us. My father flew up to the university and pledged enough money to get a science building named for old Hornsby. Coincidentally, I was let off with a stern lecture from the dean of men. I don't know how Nathan found out about it, but he did. He couldn't have been ten years old at the time; it was uncanny how he seemed to know things. My father and I had agreed to keep the whole thing from my mother. Nathan agreed as well, as long as I paid him twenty dollars a week for his silence. He wanted an airplane kit with a remote control device that cost around three hundred. It was one of those rare whims my parents had chosen not to indulge. The blackmail stopped when he had enough money for the plane. He explained it away as a gift from me, which I suppose it was." Gerald waved the memory away with a few rapid movements of his hand.

"Our relationship never really altered. When I finished school I went to work for the firm, starting as a clerk. Then my father rewarded my good behavior with a seat on the Exchange. After a few years I was one of a dozen vice-presidents. Nathan came in as a vice-president. When our father died, there was some feeling in the company that one of us should be his successor. What they wanted was a man whose business acumen they could admire and whose loyalty they could trust; they admired Nathan and trusted me. It looked like my age and years with the firm had given me the edge. Nathan privately reminded me of the college incident and some more recent pecadillos he had somehow gotten wind of and suggested I might want to step aside in his favor as it would be very embarrassing to the firm if the president's checkered past ever came under scrutiny. So you might say the presidency was my gift to him as well."

Trout was searching for some response. The man must be in shock.

Swiftly, crisply, Mildred Hornsby Adams entered the drawing room.

"Ah, Mother, this is Inspector, uh, Detective . . . Police Chief . . ."

"Trout," Trout supplied in exasperation.

"Yes, of course. He has something to tell you." With that Gerald pushed the paper into his mother's hands, nodded farewell to Trout and drew the double doors closed behind him.

Trout was furious with Gerald Adams. With himself. He watched the white-haired woman read and reread the sheet of paper. Her hands trembled, but that was the only sign of the grief Trout sensed struggling in her. He wanted to break into her thoughts and apologize profusely for the clumsy way in which she learned the news.

"Please forgive my son," she said at last as though she had been aware of Trout's thoughts even as they occurred to him.

"Forgive me for . . ."

"Why?" she interrupted, almost smiling. "Even Gerald understands such news cannot be broken gently."

Trout was sweeping his mind for appropriate words. Everything he found was formula. Then he realized this awesome old woman was searching for a way to put him at ease. His solace was useless to her, but she at least could lessen the guilt and the awkwardness of the moment for him.

"It's not that I'm a stoic. I guess I am not surprised. I love, loved my son, but I don't think I was ever blinded by my love. I love Gerald as well, though I am aware of how he must appear to you. He is a good man, but he is unable to fight for anything, against anything. I am tempted to call him the quintessential pacifist, but even pacifists fight for their right not to strike out."

A half smile again pulled at the corners of her eyes. "In the animal kingdom he could not have survived. In this rather less than human world he has had the good sense to stay within the protective territory of the she bear. You must not be so transparent, Mr. Trout. Surely that is a handicap in your work. You suspect that the responsibility for Gerald's dependence is mine, that I am one of those diligent dried-up women who make a career of refastening the umbilical cord.

"I'm wandering unforgivably. It is, of course, Nathan in whom you are interested. He was charming, quick, ambitious, appreciative of the things that cause people in this country to ambivalently bestow the title 'cultured'; and he was destructive. It wasn't just that he was ruthless in acquiring what he wanted—he was that—he was fascinated by what his ruthlessness did to others. He was always coldly curious about the effects of his actions. As far as I know, as a child Nathan never tortured cats or pulled the wings off flies. He would have seen no point to it. But had it been instrumental in getting him something he wanted, Nathan would have watched that wingless fly's dance with all the objectivity of laboratory technicians who feed nitrites to rats. That's it: Nathan made a science out of getting what he wanted."

"Mrs. Adams, I do appreciate your speaking to me of these things. It can't be easy. But this description of your son, it's not the portrait of someone who would willingly obliterate himself. It's *his* pleasure, *his* life. Why would he give it up?"

"You see, if he thought he could not continue, if he were no longer in control. Perhaps he believed that his whereabouts had been discovered. Nathan would not tolerate prison. Not couldn't, but wouldn't. Suicide is a fitting end. He was in control of his life even to the death. And there would be the added satisfaction of setting off a predictable and profound chain reaction."

"You think, then, his letter wasn't genuine? Forgive me, but when I first read it, it seemed too pat. Too standard."

"It is the letter that convinces me of the suicide. It could be classed as average, I suppose, rather human and pathetic, which Nathan was not. It was a final and, from his perspective, an amusing form of manipulation. I think he would derive great comfort from speculating on the effect this last experiment would have."

Trout put his arm around Mrs. Adam's shoulders and half carried her to the settee. They had been standing throughout the interview. To his surprise and perhaps hers, she allowed herself to be settled and patted into place.

"I think I was too old to be a mother to my sons." Her voice had fallen flat and suddenly she looked very old indeed.

Trout looked around for a bell or a buzzer and, finding it, he pressed. Less than a minute passed, but in that time Mildred

Hornsby Adams seemed to shrivel. Her eyes appeared to fade from piercing to yellowed and opaque and her skin from thin to paper. The secretary woman came through the double doors, looked once at the old woman and then turned to Trout, anxiously awaiting orders.

"Get Mrs. Adams a brandy and then call her doctor. I'll wait with her until the doctor arrives."

That night, as Trout was getting undressed, he paused to look at the woman reading in bed, head propped on one hand and pillow propping her elbow. "Enid, why is it when we think about a woman we associate her even in our thoughts with her whole name or her first name, but never just her last name?"

"Most likely it's a combination of custom and the fact that women have a history of changing their surnames. I wouldn't worry about it. Who is she, and just how much are you thinking about her?"

"The woman who saw Adams just before he jumped. And quite a bit."

"Because of what she saw or because of her?"

"Her, I guess. She seems such a catalogue of contradictions. I have trouble reading her and even more trouble interpreting my reactions to her."

"Is there any reason to believe her statement was false?"

"None. No, it's nothing like that. Move over, would you? I just have this feeling that she plays me like a piano. She's imperious and feminine at the same time."

"Feminine? Now what's that supposed to mean?"

"I don't know. It's a stupid word, yes. But I can't seem to find another that will do as well."

"I'm sorry. Go on."

"I found myself grateful that Adams chose to kill himself while she was passing, that this stroke of fortune brought her to me. This evening I caught myself growing irate at the notion that I would otherwise never have met her."

"Sounds like simple infatuation to me. You did say at dinner that she's wealthy, intelligent, cultured and good-looking."

"Yes."

"There you are. Everyman's dream made flesh. You find yourself attracted to her and, being as monogomous as a parrot, you can't be unfaithful even in your thoughts. So you have to clothe her allure in some profound and preternatural rationale. Stop looking for justifications and accept that even your opinions are not entirely formed above the belt."

"You're probably right."

Trout was inevitably catalogued by others as a nice man. He accepted that assessment. He loved his wife; he supposed that she was cleverer than he but the thought did not rankle; he did the dishes and shared in the other mindless household tasks without resentment or a feeling of beneficence. He loved his children; he was sometimes rather surprised that he had been dealt three daughters but he did not long for a male heir; while he enjoyed them, especially now that they were beyond the standard childhood diseases and for the most part self-sufficient, he did not dread the time when they would leave him. He had friends; there were persons beyond the limits of Fells Harbor who thought first of him in their good times and bad; people felt they knew him despite his inability, or his aversion, to indulge in self-revelation. He took his job seriously; he was satisfied with his work though he found no glory in it; he took comfort in the notion that he was not a parasite, assuring himself that his job served a real need instead of creating one.

He was in some respects ill suited for his job. At least his background was an unconventional one for a county sheriff. He had struggled through undergraduate school at MIT, on scholarship and burdened with a series of part-time jobs, only to discover in his junior year that he hated engineering and barely tolerated engineers. He graduated with a liberal arts degree and a major in English. From MIT. That marked the beginning of his career as a square peg in a round hole.

He remet Enid in graduate school. She was in history, and he had embraced the eighteenth-century British wits—Boswell, Johnson, Goldsmith, and Sheridan. He and Enid had maintained a nodding acquaintance through childhood, growing up not ten miles apart but separated by the deeply etched social lines drawn in a small town. For all their seeming differences, their shared geography bound them together in defense against the much colder climate of the Eastern university.

Enid had known precisely what she wanted: her doctorate in American history and a position in a small New England college. And marriage to Trout. They were wed, and she became pregnant. In that order.

Trout seemed bent on deciding his interests through a process of elimination. He abandoned his devotion to literature and was mailing applications to law schools when Enid was stricken with a case of prepartum depression.

They were living in shabby, prefabricated postwar married-student housing. She was due to deliver in a month and had decided to take a leave of absence from school. Trout had just withdrawn from the English department, so even his meager salary as a teaching assistant would no longer be trickling in. Hanging over them like an unpaid bill was the certainty that they would have to give up their grim little apartment to tuition paying students.

Trout came home one afternoon from a judicious shopping spree at Goodwill with the disassembled parts of a much used crib poking out of the VW only to find that Enid had neatly boxed all their belongings. She insisted she was going to have her baby in clean, bucolic Fells Harbor whether he accompanied her or not. Trout couldn't shake her resolve, but he didn't try very hard. There was nothing at present to hold them in Boston and the move would only be temporary, just until after the baby was born. They'd been there ever since.

Enid had watched him unblinkingly for fully three minutes while he seemed to stare at a crack in the plaster by the window. "She must be quite fascinating," she said at last.

"She is," he said eagerly, relieved to be talking of her again. "I'd like you to meet her. Really."

"I don't think so. I'm quite wonderful and all, but I have an idea that in a side-by-side comparison I'd be found wanting. Has this Circe a name?"

"Eve Galatea."

"You see how pale Enid Trout sounds by comparison. I'm beginning to take this personally."

Trout laughed, relaxing finally. "You're never jealous."

"Ah, you're talking about the past. I've never ruled out the possibility. Is she Greek, then?"

"Why Greek? Your catty reference to Circe?"

"No, dullard, Galatea. That was the name of the statue created by Pygmalion that he fell hopelessly in love with. The gods took pity on him and turned her marbled limbs into flesh."

"Some historical background for your theory? Foreshadowing? You've already convinced me that Eve Galatea is the embodiment of the woman of my dreams. Do you want me to believe that despite seemingly overwhelming barriers she's also accessible—that I can have my dream and eat it, too?"

Enid deftly lobbed a pillow at Trout's offending mouth. "You'd never let yourself get away with it; the Puritan ethic is too strong in you. After one tryst I'd be tripping over guilty proofs. You'd take to reading Edith Hamilton; you'd hum snatches from *My Fair Lady;* you'd be bringing bottles of retsina and ouzo home. If only you were a Catholic you'd have the satisfaction of confessing your lascivious thoughts and the comfort of at least having sinned in your soul if not in her bed."

"Not a chance for me, then?"

"None."

"My only course is to renounce her."

"Absolutely."

"I'd like to," suddenly serious. "There's something. I don't know. I can't clear her from my mind."

CHAPTER 3

Things were moving along apace now. The work that fell to Trout's office was becoming more and more routine. For all practical purposes the investigation was out of his hands. There was to be an inquest, but no one, least of all Trout, expected that to be anything but a ceremonial nod to form.

His staff's reactions to the presence of the FBI and the watchdogs of the press had been predictable and therefore mildly amusing.

Homer was resentful that the FBI had been summoned and that their arrival had dissolved his moment of glory. He assiduously tried to remedy that by cultivating connections with the media. The few terse press releases from his office Trout issued through Homer. Trout considered purchasing a scrapbook for him but suspected the gesture would be a duplication and feared that Homer would not be insulted.

Agronski was the antithesis of Homer. He was very ambitious but only within the context of his own job. He subscribed to legal journals, read volumes on criminology, and was responsible for their relatively sophisticated lab equipment. He wanted to do his job expertly. He wasn't often challenged—traffic violations and littering were the commonest offenses. However, because of its location, Fells Harbor was not the typical provincial sleepy town. It was a watering place for the idle and the rich and the idle rich. The seasonal upsurge in crime helped keep Agronski going.

He had even worked on two murder cases. One had been open and shut—a young woman who confessed to killing her father-in-law for criticizing her cooking. The other had been long and involved but never tedious for Agronski: by day he did detective and lab work; by night he constructed psychological profiles and formulated methods and motives.

Agronski would not have been uncomfortable in hearing his profession likened to that of an artist. He would immediately downplay his own talents, asserting with boyish seriousness that, while he might never rise to the caliber of the Old Masters, he could and would continue to refine his technique.

The presence of the reporters grieved him. They interrupted his work; they interrupted each other. They were bored and boringly determined to unearth something worth copy between now and the inquest. He wished the town's liquor licenses were more liberal, nursing the conviction that if the bars were open continuously the members of the fourth estate would not make their headquarters at his elbow.

He was, however, delighted with the federal investigators milling around and passing through. Trout was somewhat flabbergasted at overhearing a snatch of intense conversation between Agronski and some FBI consultant on the subject of carbon dating. Agronski would be prepared to solve the murder of Cro-Magnon Man if the need arose. Oddly enough, he perceived each of these interlopers as having definite knowledge from which he could learn. More odd still, Trout thought, he probably did.

Agronski had just brought Trout the FBI report on Eve Galatea. Not much there. Born in Ohio, of all places. Never married. No family remaining. A small-scale heiress. No permanent address for her until she settled in Boston about a year ago, though settled was hardly the word to describe her lifestyle. Neighbors in the surrounding apartments were questioned, and they sketched the outline of a recluse. Eve Galatea was seldom seen. In the first months of her tenancy she spent most of her time in travel, communicating with the building manager via the written word about rent, spraying for crawling insects and malfunction of her central air conditioning unit. Later she spent more time at her apartment but was recognizable to her neighbors only by her large sunglasses, larger hats, and her utter remoteness. Being aloof in Boston is not something that should be manifest—it's almost a requirement for residency. Eve Galatea had been unusually unapproachable. Her neighbors, who had little enough commerce with each other, referred to her among themselves as "Garbo." She seldom went out and had no visitors, of that the security guard was sure. A cloister of one, thought Trout.

In recent months she emerged from her cocoon, almost literally. She had shed some of the layers of clothing that seemed to protect her from the rest of the world and was even seen hatless. She exchanged politenesses in the elevator and the lobby.

The thrust of the report—the only thing, in fact, that was of concern to everyone else on the case—was that there was nothing to connect her with Nathan Adams. The possibility of her collusion was the single element that could transform the suicide into murder or a charade enacted to terminate the search for Adams. The paper concluded that there was no reason to believe they had ever come in contact. There was a footnote as to her character that amused Trout. The agent who had interrogated Eve Galatea found her "forthright and scrupulous. Unlikely to engage in any act of deception." An elegant girl scout, Trout smiled. It seems her appeal is universal.

The pressure was off now. Even though the money had yet to be recovered, at least Adams wasn't out spending it. Trout had commented to Enid that what he found most peculiar was

Adams' failure to indicate the location of his cache. The farewell letter would have been the appropriate vehicle, he thought.

"You mean he should have made a clean breast of it to insure his place in the hereafter?"

"Um," responded Trout.

"Seems to me from your own characterization of the man that that's the last thing he'd do. Probably his chief consolation was the thought of you all scurrying around trying to find the loot. A few weeks of determined effort are indicated. After that I think the money should be written off. He'll either have made it easy to find or impossible."

"Of course," said Trout. "I describe him to you and you understand him better than I do. Intuition?"

"Raw intelligence. What I'm really curious about is where and how he spent the last fourteen months."

"Let me know when you unravel that one. I've been living with it for more than a year now myself."

"Well, he had enough money to be anywhere doing anything."

"As you say. But how do you purchase invisibility?"

Trout drove out to the Hornsby house. It fell to him to check Eve Galatea's identity with the family. Another formality. It was suggested to Trout that his presence might make it easier, a familiar face and all that. He was doubtful, but at least the subject of discussion was one he could warm to.

This time he was met at the door by Gerald, who seemed quite relaxed as he led Trout to the now familiar-feeling drawing room. Even his appearance was altered. He was dressed comfortably, but Trout could hardly believe the word casual was applicable. His clothes looked like they had been carefully pieced together on a window mannequin in Saks and Gerald had purchased the whole package right down to the tasseled loafers. The effect was of the Young Executive at Leisure—one hand around a glass of Harvey's Bristol Cream, the other on the corporate ladder.

Trout inquired after his mother,whom Gerald declared to be fully recovered. They chatted a bit about the press coverage and the coming inquest. As though we were equals, mused Trout. As though we came from a similar background and as though I credited him with a grain of common sense or sensitivity. Finally Trout asked him if he knew a woman named Eve Galatea or of a woman matching her description who might have known his brother. Gerald didn't reflect long: he knew of no such person.

Trout wanted to ask the same question of Mrs. Adams and the young secretary. Gerald assured him that his mother was certainly able to see him. He would bring her down presently and in the meantime send Gretchen Bergstrom to him.

Gerald was gone barely long enough for Trout to begin analyzing the change in his demeanor when Gretchen paced into the room. She did not linger outside the door as Trout had vaguely imagined she might from their previous encounter. She was withdrawn and self-effacing, but of course there had to be some measure of efficiency to qualify her for her employment. She had been told to present herself to Trout for questioning. A command performance, so to speak.

"I believe you wished to question me?"

She was all business now. He had better get on with it or in her thoroughness she would supply the queries as well as the responses.

"Have you ever heard the name Eve Galatea?"

"No. Only from what's been in the papers, I mean."

Trout offered a physical description.

"I don't believe I am acquainted with anyone of such appearance."

"I thought it possible that in your position you might know if Nathan Adams had any relationship with Miss Galatea."

"I was never secretary to Mr. Adams. I am Mrs. Adams' personal secretary." Her face was flushed with color save two white lines on either side of her nose. "I was not privy to his engagement calendar, if that's what you mean. I don't know why you would question me about his private life." She pounded each "I" at the beginning of her sentences as though striking herself.

Trout was surprised but dismissed her with a throwaway "Thank you."

At the door she wheeled to face him. "If you're trying to prove he committed suicide over some woman, it's preposterous."

She left him trying to determine which among the range of emotions that colored her parting speech predominated. He detected shades of love, jealousy, protectiveness, anger, and reproach. All that repressed feeling for one man. From a most unexpected source. Though she had stood before him not more than five minutes past, Trout found that already his memory could not trace her features. They blurred into one another. She was a cop's nemesis: a totally nondescript person. Except her voice. There was a jarring quality to it as though all her personality had to find expression there and the facets coming together produced not a symphony but an embarrassing dissonance. It was too raw.

Trout had, after his conversation with Gerald, concluded that the family was not as bizarre as the circumstances of his acquaintance conspired to make it appear. He was impressed by the formidable yet vulnerable personage of the dowager, but now his chief thought was of the harvest to be reaped here by a psychiatrist—a convention of psychologists, an army of family therapists. Freudians would gorge themselves on the mother-sons relationships, and primal scream therapy would be just the thing for greyish Gretchen.

Mildred Hornsby Adams came into the room on the arm of her remaining son. She looked older than she had at the outset of their prior interview, and she supported herself with a cane grasped in her free hand. But there was no air of the invalid about her. She had been wounded, yes, but not mortally. There was still an aura of grace, even of power, around her. Trout was reminded of some other woman, some shadow that haunted his thoughts when he was in her presence, but prod as he might, his brain would yield no features, no particulars. He ascribed the sensation to *déjà vu*.

"Gerald tells me you wish to question me about the young woman who witnessed Nathan's death. I'm perfectly up to it, so please don't concern yourself about that. Before you begin, however, I should like to thank you for your kindness to us, to me, particularly, at our last meeting. I have thought of you often in the intervening days."

Trout was embarrassed. To cover it he lowered his eyes as the flush rose up his neck and in doing so he saw that his left pant leg had ridden up, exposing his calf, which only served to heighten his embarrassment. These were the situations in which he never had the right words. In the face of someone else's gratitude, admiration, sorrow, or shame he was as awkward as the man in the three-piece suit who discovers he has stepped squarely into a mound of dog shit. He knew better than to murmur something self-deprecating, as that would only lead to further plaudits. He said tersely, "I am glad I did not make the situation any more difficult for you."

Mrs. Adams smiled benevolently at his discomfiture and eased him into a discussion of the subject of his current visit. "Does this woman purport to be an acquaintance of mine?"

"Not at all. Unlikely as it seems even to us, we are examining the possibility that she is in some way connected with your son Nathan as other than a witness."

"A conspirator?"

"As I said: unlikely."

"Is she from one of the coastal towns? I can't recall from what I've read."

"No, she's from Boston. Vacationing." Trout described her at length, stopping himself when he heard the enthusiasm in his voice, and abruptly asked about Nathan's relationships with women.

"I really can't think of anyone," Mrs. Adams considered after a thoughtful pause, "who even remotely resembles your awesome Amazon."

"You've probably hit upon the precise key to her otherworldly charms. A direct descendent of an Amazon queen. Not too farfetched, since she is Greek."

"Greek, really?"

"An assumption based solely on her surname. I would guess some generations removed."

"And the name? I don't recall hearing it."

"Galatea."

"Galatea?"

"Eve Galatea."

"Eve Galatea?"

"Mother," Gerald broke in, "you're going to force me to make some miserable pun about the echo you're creating and the Greek nymph of the same name."

"Of course, Gerald," she said absently.

Trout watched the puzzlement etch a frown on the old woman's face. "You do know her or recognize the name?"

"I feel as if I should, yet I am entirely certain that I have neither seen nor heard of her before. Peculiar feeling." She shook it off.

"Perhaps you're just recalling the Pygmalion myth."

"Perhaps it's that. I suppose so. Anyway, if my son knew Miss Galatea covertly I would be much surprised. He was not a hedonist." Trout looked up sharply and she smiled. "The young woman would not thank me for the way that last statement followed the other. I just mean that while Nathan was resolute in satisfying his appetites, those appetites were of rather a pristine nature. Despite his cultural and social activities, he led what would be regarded by most as a monastic life."

Gerald had been thinking during his mother's assessment and he added, "I think it's very unlikely that Nathan had a relationship with this woman, and impossible unless it occurred in the year or so following his disappearance."

"We can rule that out. Her life is an open book during that period without any men at all punctuating it."

"You see," Gerald explained, "I really can't conceive of Nathan engaging in a clandestine affair. He only found romance in a painting or a rare book—he thrived in a very rarefied atmosphere. My mother used the word monastic. I think solipsistic is more accurate."

Mrs. Adams nodded silent assent.

Trout thanked them, half rising from his chair, and then gave way to his curiosity. "Were you both aware that Gretchen was in love with Nathan?"

"We were very careful not to let on," Mrs. Adams sighed. "I did come close to dismissing her. I spoke of my diminishing need for her services and suggested that I might find her a more stimulating and lucrative position with one of my friends, that kind of thing. She looked like a wounded wild creature with demented eyes, pleading to stay, offering to work for only her keep. She was so pathetic and I judged, perhaps unwisely, that the damage had been done, that she was quite unfit to go elsewhere. Gerald and I felt we owed her some kind of shelter and, despite her obsession for Nathan, she really is a fine secretary."

"She told you she loved Nathan?" Gerald queried in disbelief.

"No. I'm sure she would have denied it adamantly, but it was painfully evident. Of course, you understand her better than I do, but I think she is walking a very thin line and her balance is none too good."

"We seem to reserve our breakdowns for your visits," Gerald said.

"I'm being presumptuous," Trout apologized.

It was Gerald's turn to reproach himself. "I'm glad you spoke. We are too inclined to view Gretchen through a veil of tolerance. We might tolerate her right into a collapse. If one fleeting encounter was enough to convince an outsider, er, a more objective viewer, that she's in need of help, then it seems time that we see she gets it."

Mrs. Adams elaborated. "When Gretchen came to us she was quite young and, I think, a bit in awe of much we tend to take for granted. Very impressionable. But she was remarkably bright, and I considered myself fortunate to have her in my employ. She took over a number of duties which advancing age made me only too glad to relinquish." She paused to tighten the thread of her narrative. "Nathan as well noticed her brightness. That combined with her youth made her an attractive protege.

He took it upon himself to introduce her innate discrimination to the acquired tastes—ranging from caviar to opera, and ultimately to Nathan himself."

"She was a willing pupil, but he succeeded best in the last category," Gerald said heavily. "Enough so that the nature of his attention changed from a teacher's to a tormentor's."

"He tested Gretchen continuously. To see what her affection would bear," explained the mother. "I'm afraid it was rather degrading for her."

"Every time he would humiliate her, she would accept it as the price she must pay for the company of her Henry Higgins," Gerald said. "Each time she failed to protest, his annoyance increased and so did his cruelty."

"Why didn't he just pull away?" Trout asked. "Unless you're saying that in his own way he was in love with her."

Mrs. Adams and Gerald exchanged a glance, each ready to defer to the other. It was Gerald who finally spoke. "That's not an emotion Nathan was capable of. In fact, I don't think he suffered emotions at all, not even anger. Pleasure and displeasure, yes, but those were abstract reactions, not feelings. I think he enjoyed plumbing the depths of Gretchen's worship—it was a fascinating game," Gerald coughed up a dry laugh, "like buying on margin. But even that wasn't the chief reason for continuing the involvement—the relationship was convenient for him."

Mildred Hornsby Adams took her cue. "Nathan had no particular interest in women as . . . partners. Nor in men," she added hastily.

"Put succinctly," Gerald interjected, "he was asexual as well as amoral."

"But society often expects a man to be in the company of a woman," Mrs. Adams resumed. "Gretchen filled a dual role in that she, well, complemented him socially, almost like a part of his wardrobe, gave him a finished appearance, and in that she served effectively to keep other women at bay."

Whether because he judged the explanation to be complete or because the topic disturbed him, Gerald brought the conversation back to a more impersonal exchange. "Can you tell me if the date set for the inquest is definite? I intend to be there, but I also have some business to attend to in New York."

"Gerald has accepted Nathan's position in the company. For months now the board has been after him and only yesterday he made the decision."

Trout blinked in disbelief. Gerald did indeed seem radically changed in his demeanor, and most markedly in his bearing toward his mother, but to envision him as one of the moguls of Wall Street forced a major revision of the man's abilities and ambitions.

"The inquest is certain to be held on Friday. The announcement was given out in a press release this morning. Except for the sensational nature of the death itself and the history of your brother, it should be pretty clear plodding. I mean there's no new evidence. The outcome isn't in dispute."

"Nevertheless, I think it's important that we be there," Gerald spoke quietly.

Trout took some tea and his leave.

"Enid, I want desperately to smuggle you into the Hornsby house."

"You only have to mention the place and lust fills my soul. Some pretty fine pieces come my way, but they're reproductions. Old reproductions: you know, 'in the style of Hepplewhite' or whatever. Hell, I'd polish their furniture gratis just for the opportunity to run my hands over it."

"You really are monomaniacal. You're babbling about bric-a-brac . . ."

"Bric-a-brac!"

". . . and I'm talking about the most fascinating menage since the household of Oedipus."

"Babbling!"

"You're slow on the uptake. Dense like oak or mahogany. Thousands of years ago some Olympian resident would have been moved by your unfulfilled state and, as was their wont with virginal wood nymphs, rooted you to the ground. Just think, you might have been the first sequoia."

"Undoubtedly I would have been the first enid tree, subject to Dutch enid disease."

"You could have had the thrill of being hewn and carved, of

being transformed. You might today be one of those pieces you rave about—an eighteenth-century armoire, say."

"Gad, egad, and gadzooks, man, I should hope not. Nobody takes care of such things anymore. Before the industrial revolution anyone who could afford to own passable furniture could afford to keep help to tend it. Have you ever thought why I haven't cluttered this house with my fabulous finds?"

"Greed. Filthy lucre, as they say."

"Yes, well, aside from that."

"Avarice."

"You're repeating yourself."

"Enlighten me."

"I don't have the patience or the inclination to keep them properly oiled or caressed. These days to furnish your house with antiques demands ceaseless devotion. I do not want to be the high priestess of my home."

"Pithy, that last line."

"Thank you." Trout had moved around behind her and was lightly and repeatedly kissing the back of her neck. "What were you saying?"

"Mmm."

"No. I mean before. About the Adams clan."

"Not important."

"Don't make me wheedle. Tell."

"Sweet and salty."

"What?"

"Your neck."

"If you don't talk you'll be put on a diet."

"Withholding. The basest form of manipulation."

"Whatever works," she shrugged.

"Fish." Trout dropped his arms and settled on the couch lighting a cigarette. "First you show no interest and then when I'm well involved in another subject. . . ."

"You sham. You're panting to tell me the latest installment in the saga of the eccentric and distinguished archduchess and her middle-aged milksop son."

"That's what's so fantastic. The stage is the same; the actors are the same; but all the characters have been changed. Oh, yes, and a bit part has been expanded.

"Mildred Hornsby Adams is, well, not broken but softened. That's the word. She actually deferred to Gerald now and then. And Gerald—it's as though he finally accepted the role he was destined to play. Instead of merely renting his name for the letterhead he is assuming the board presidency of the Hornsby firm. That signifies. Not only is it a show of guts—sorry—but for him to have been offered the position indicates that he has far more in the way of ability and acumen than I ever would have credited him with."

"I have always felt a secret affinity with late bloomers."

"Your day will come."

"Shut up and go on."

"And as for the walk-on, the briskly efficient secretary, she is as hung up on Nathan Adams as you are on nineteenth-century commodes."

"Did she say so?"

"She'd never admit it, but I drew fire when I asked about the possibility of any relationship between him and Eve Galatea."

"Any substance to that?"

"No connection at all as far as I can tell."

"Pity. They would have made quite a pair."

"What do you mean by that?" Trout's voice had an edge to it.

"Look at what they would have had in common: a high regard for money, unerring good taste, interest in the arts, and a general superiority to mere mortals. A striking couple. Everyone would have said so."

"You don't know what you're talking about."

"I see. My turn to change the subject." Enid hesitated, then crossed the room and dropped beside him on the couch. She began fumbling with his shirt buttons as she nibbled in the vicinity of his ear. His face remained stony.

A minute or so passed, then, "I have a headache," Trout said.

CHAPTER 4

The inquest was held in the auditorium of the county's Elizabeth Cady Stanton High School. The VFW hall wasn't large enough, and the basement of the Episcopal church was being repainted.

Trout blinked to clear his vision, then realized that the haze was in the air. It was an uncommonly hot day without the respite of a sea breeze. He had awakened that morning with the feeling that something was missing. He didn't probe this realization too deeply out of a sense of caution. He wasn't prepared to deal with any great lack he might discover in himself, so he shelved the impression. The feeling doubled back on him now, accompanied by a flash of recognition. It was just that there was no salt in the air, except perhaps the salt of human perspiration. It was the sharp cleanness of taking in the ocean with each breath that he missed.

He looked around the room, which was rank with the motionless air of the overclothed bodies. He was grateful that attendance at the inquest was less than half the number he had anticipated. But then, he thought, it's the heat that's kept the rest away, and I'd rather be rubbing elbows than surreptitiously trying to keep my clothes from sticking to my body.

Trout had asked Enid over breakfast if she was interested in viewing the proceedings, and she had demurred, offering too many reasons why she needed to be elsewhere. They had been handling each other with politeness these last few days. Trout knew from experience that such carefulness in their relationship was a bleakly ominous sign. But he wasn't going to analyze that, either.

With half-closed eyes he noted that all the necessary participants were present and had arrived early. That was satisfying, and he felt a small surge of gratitude toward all the principal players. His brow furrowed when his glance rested on Gretchen. Why couldn't he recall her last name? Why did they let her come? He had asked precisely that of Gerald Adams when the latter had joined him for a cigarette outside on the steps after settling his mother and her secretary in the hall. Gerald shrugged his resignation, saying that she was determined to attend and that the doctor had no objections. They couldn't very well lock her into the turret, and a measure of that kind was what was required to ensure her absence.

Besides, Gerald had said, his mother thought that this might make Gretchen more resigned to Nathan's death. Since the body hadn't been recovered and they were unable to take refuge in the mind-dulling ceremonies of wake and funeral, the formality of the inquest might serve to introduce the cathartic process of mourning.

Trout had felt a twinge of anger at Gerald's coolness. Here was a man who accepted the fact of his brother's death, yet there wasn't a trace of mourning about him—not in the expensive summer-weight suit that hung perfectly on his large frame, not in his salon-styled hair, not in the crispness of his salmon-colored shirt. The rich don't sweat, thought Trout. Or maybe it's genetic: that thin blue blood trickling through the veins. Maybe he does feel grief but his blood prevents him from showing that as well.

No, he surmised, the present Gerald may have risen from the

ashes of the burnt-out creature he had met on the day of
Nathan's death, his emotions and ambitions might have been
transformed, but he was still as transparent as he had been that
morning, still unable to misrepresent himself, undesirous of
doing so.

He doesn't mourn his brother, reasoned Trout, and why
should he? The man was some kind of monster that only a
mother and a slightly demented secretary could love. He's not
guilty of anything, and I admire him for not feeling guilty. Had
the circumstances been different—no note, no witness—I and a
score of other people, not to mention the press, would probably
be trying to tuck him away in a cell for the murder of his
brother.

Despite the promptness of all those who were to give testimony, the inquest began late. Trout suspected that the county
coroner had been struggling in the men's room with his hair-
piece, which was perched slightly awry. Vanity, thy name is
elected official.

After a few introductory remarks and the standard explanation of the purpose of an inquest—to determine the manner of
death and whether further court action was required, but that
this was a body whose function was to recommend without
onus of proof as to the guilt of any particular party—Trout was
called.

He recited that morning's events, responded to the questions
put to him and stepped down to make way for the trail of
experts. It was a rather ho-hum affair for the reporters: no
recently uncovered facts, no contradictory data and, by the by,
no lead on the location of the embezzled money. The outcome
was obvious before it began and most were just hanging on
waiting for Eve Galatea's testimony, hoping she'd provide
something quotable.

Trout didn't have a chance to speak with her before the
proceedings began. A sullen resentment stirred in him that was
vaguely inspired by the swarm of reporters clustered around
her. Once he had pinpointed her presence, his gaze wandered
restively until it again settled on her. Drifting into a kind of

reverie, he futilely sought the one adjective that best suited her.
It wasn't beautiful or breathtaking or glamorous; it wasn't
anything so hackneyed or superficial. The word probably hadn't
yet been coined.

She was quite good on the stand, not the least bit sensational,
but matter-of-fact with a tinge of regret shading her voice. She
was suited and hatted again and yet looked more comfortable
than the young woman seated next to him in a sleeveless
abbreviated dress, with bare legs and rubber thongs on her feet.
Trout, whose shirt collar now adhered damply to his neck, was
reconsidering the relationship between adaptability to climatic
extremes and annual income while his eyes remained fixed on
Eve Galatea.

So he was as startled as everyone else when she had completed her testimony, risen from the chair, and a voice from
behind him shrieked, "How could you?" Those tones were
unmistakable. He turned just in time to see Gretchen, who had
lurched to her feet, faint awkwardly to the floor, mouth still
open and the words still reverberating in the steaming air.
Trout swiveled his glance back to the makeshift witness stand
to discover Eve Galatea's eyes searching for his, a bewildered
plea manifest in them.

The coroner, tugging abstractedly at his toupee, adjourned
the proceedings for one hour.

Well, Trout thought glumly, that will give them something
to wire the home office about.

A lot was accomplished in that hour. Mrs. Hornsby Adams'
physician was summoned and arrived almost instantly to everyone's amazement.

Trout's cynicism toward the medical profession led him into
deliberations as to the weight of wealthy patients and retainers
versus loyalty and the Hippocratic oath.

George Cox, the medical examiner, had failed to revive
Gretchen, but the good doctor succeeded almost immediately.
Perhaps that was because he was not too sophisticated to resort
to a glass of cold water dashed in the face, or perhaps it was

because the medical examiner was not in the habit of reviving bodies. Generally speaking, attempts to do so would have been much frowned upon in his line of work.

Trout was plotting out a modern version of Dr. Frankenstein when Gretchen finally found her voice. She hadn't retrieved it entirely, however, as the sounds came out as indistinct gurglings. That could be attributed to residual effects of her unorthodox baptism. He leaned closer. After a full minute he realized she was mumbling one word over and over—"abomination." Gretchen was given an injection of something, surely a sedative, as she stopped speaking and slumped back into the arms of Gerald Adams.

After a brief exchange with the coroner, Mother and son left, the latter supporting almost the full weight of Gretchen. Trout saw the soundness of this maneuver. It served the dual purpose of marking their concern over the overwrought employee, and as their flight had the aura of medical necessity about it, they were left virtually unmolested by reporters.

This left the doctor and Trout to make explanations to the coroner, A. J. Henson, whose expression failed to mask his irritation. Trout was jabbing his memory, trying to recall the doctor's name when Henson barked, "Well, Dr. Cutter?" A glimmer of relief flickered over Trout's face as he realized he had never before heard the physician addressed. Cutter. A name to inspire confidence in one's sawbones. Trout recalled meeting a profoundly offensive Klansman in Mississippi who bore the surname Lynch. Perhaps his own hatred for fishing was nothing more than a small rebellion against the Fates.

"I have been treating Miss Bergstrom for an emotional condition these past few days. I was called in by Mrs. Adams, whom I have attended during the summer months for many years now."

Trout didn't know if it was Cutter's diction or his buttoned-down formality that made him sound as though he were reading from a prepared speech. "It was partly at my instigation," Trout broke in. "Even to me it was obvious she was unstrung by Nathan Adams' suicide."

"Get to the point. They were lovers?"

"Only she. Unrequited."

"What's her fix on the Galatea woman?"

Trout bristled, unreasonably, he knew. "Nothing there. She had never even heard of her until I mentioned the name. Of that I'm sure."

"I feel responsible for this. I've had contact with Gretchen Bergstrom for a period of, I guess it must be seven years now," Cutter said with a surgical precision, "and I have naturally formed opinions about her personality. She is intelligent and capable enough that I was mildly surprised at her staying on with Mrs. Adams. Not that the work was unpleasant or her employer uncongenial, but that she was content to remain a social secretary. Eventually I learned of her infatuation with Nathan Adams. I don't know if that caused her problems or if it was some lack in her that led to the obsession, and it's pointless for me to speculate. I'm no psychiatrist, just a simple GP."

Like hell, Trout thought, probing his conviction that Cutter was meticulously choosing his words. Trout expressed his grudging admiration and Cutter acknowledged it, each with a slight nod of the head.

"Let's hear about your responsibility for her outburst," the coroner put in peevishly.

"Miss Bergstrom was adamant about attending the inquest. Mrs. Adams and her son were unable to dissuade her, so they consulted me. I encouraged them to let her come. I believe I convinced Mrs. Adams that the finality of these proceedings might enable Miss Bergstrom to begin a long process of heal-ing." Here Cutter halted briefly, consciously stemming the fervor that was rising in his voice. "My judgment was wrong. She should have been prevented from coming. But for your purposes, it is enough to say that her ability to discern what is real from what she wants or what she fears is completely unreliable."

"Meaning?" said Henson.

"Meaning," returned Trout, "that except for what she's read in the papers or heard on the eleven o'clock news, Gretchen, uh, Bergstrom has no idea who Eve Galatea is or what, if anything, she might have done. She's jealous of Adams' reputation. Wants to protect his shrine from the preying female. Ha. It's totally irrational and our hour recess is just about over."

Henson gave Trout a warning glance, but seemed convinced that there were no new dimensions to the case. He reconvened the inquest, calling Dr. Cutter to explain the inadvisability of considering Gretchen Bergstrom's accusation as more than an unfounded outburst resulting from the combined effects of emotional instability and the prodigious heat. The coroner cautioned the reporters present not to make headlines out of an unfortunate young woman's hysteria. Things continued informally, and the hearing came to a rapid close. The verdict of the coroner's jury: Nathan Edmund Adams, thirty-three years old, did on August 11 willfully and with premeditation take his own life.

The only surprise Trout felt was at his own disappointment that it was all over. In the past he had sometimes experienced a letdown when a case he had been working on was closed. He assumed it was the stimulation that he missed. This time he had to recognize that what was stimulating him was Eve Galatea, and what he was going to miss was the possibility of seeing her again.

He caught up with her at the door and gently touched her elbow. She turned and looked at him expectantly. Trout suggested coffee and she nodded. He kept his hand on her elbow and guided her the block and a half to a dimly lit tavern that served the best coffee and the only decent corned beef sandwich in town.

Their journey had been entirely wordless. They sat in a booth close to the entrance—Trout's concession to feeling guilty about being anywhere but his office in her company. She remained silent, shaking her head in negation when the waitress appeared and Trout praised the quality of the corned beef. He ordered a sandwich for himself anyway. He hadn't eaten any breakfast and, besides, eating would somehow reinforce the casual nature of this conversation.

His glance, which had been nervously ricocheting around the room, finally settled on her face. A fine face. And it was staring into his. This is it, he thought. I make my move right now. One gesture. A few words.

"Would you pass the mustard?"

Eve Galatea laughed and the tension was gone. Relief washed over Trout and dissolved the hardness in his stomach. He was glad that the choosing was over even while he regretted his choice. And even then he wondered whose decision it really had been.

"Looked like it might get exciting there for a minute. The only thing more palpable than the heat in that room was the anticipation that Gretchen, uh, Bergstrom was going to reveal the lurid details of your past."

"You won't consider it an overstatement if I say that was an awkward moment?"

"The coroner, Henson, handled it well, though. I don't think you'll figure in any sensational headlines, except maybe on the eighth page of a supermarket-cum-movie-magazine-type rag." She grimaced. "Cutter really clinched it for you. It's lucky he surfaced as quickly as he did, or you'd have been back on the stand with precisely the same story but a suddenly hostile audience. Most people hate an open and shut case, anyway. In a community like this they feel particularly cheated when the festivities cease—we don't have much in the way of theatre.

"It's funny how people fail to realize how devastated an individual can be by merely being suspected of something. Especially an unnamed something.

"If all the facts point to an easy conclusion and dramatic alternatives aren't explored in the papers and the courts, the theory is the cop hasn't done his—or her, excuse me—job. Stupidity or corruption. Especially in our centers of civilization, i.e., the big cities. Unless you catch some bullets, which impresses everyone with your diligence and sincerity, the only attention you receive is going to carry an accusation of being either dumb or venal. Brutal, too. I forgot that. What kind of populace do we have if the only people we can find to police us are sadistic greedy morons, if such . . ." She arrested his fingers on the fourth attempt to light the match. Her hand lingered over his briefly, then came away holding the matchbook. She struck the match, lit his cigarette and waited.

He was subdued now. "I guess you could make a good case for possession. I came close just now to saying, 'I don't know what's got into me' and you were looking like, 'He's not himself.'" He paused. "I don't talk about it much, but I do feel it. On a percentage basis alone, there are a lot of priests out there that I would like to tell to go to hell; most doctors should be ordered to drop dead; we could halve the criminal population by doing away with the legal profession; but I've met a lot of cops I wouldn't mind getting drunk with."

"What brought this on now? None of it particularly applies to the Adams case."

He brooded over that a while. "I guess I feel defensive about my chosen profession in your presence." He said this simply, without apology.

"Do I do that?"

"It's not you; it's me. I guess, and it's only a guess, that while I'm playing defender of the world's police for you I'm trying to convince myself that I'm just as interesting as anybody else and better than, say, the president of a brokerage firm who absconds with the loot and ends up in the ocean."

"Speaking of oceans, you're fishing. I'm not going to sit here and toss you compliments, but I would like to express some gratitude."

"Delighted."

"You were praising the coroner and that doctor for not letting that young woman's explosion evolve into some kind of scandal with me as the central figure. I suspect you had a heavy hand in that."

"Not really."

"You're impossible. Less than a minute ago I was afraid that anything I said would be construed as damning with too faint praise. Accept my thanks. It's not something that I give easily."

There was an audible silence. "I suppose you'll be leaving now," Trout said without inflection.

"Not yet. In a few days, perhaps."

"Oh?"

"I might as well do some sketches and a little painting as long as I'm settled in. That's what I came for." The look with which she favored him was a clear enunciation of that not being what she was staying for.

Trout paid the check. "I won't say good-bye, then."

That night at dinner Trout regaled the family with the details of the inquest. He enacted the major roles, doing a fair imitation of Cutter, and his performance as Henson the Vain won for him the last barbecued sparerib and spontaneous applause.

Enid appeared to be enjoying his one-man show as much as the girls, and she seemed to take as little notice as they when he inserted the statement that he had seen Eve Galatea at the tavern following the inquest. He couldn't bring himself to admit that she had been present at his invitation. He told himself that he wasn't hiding anything, because there really wasn't anything to hide.

Then Enid contributed to the general high spirits by recounting the tale of a purchase she had tried to make that day. She had driven inland to a farm that must have been well over a hundred years old. Its boards and shingles seemed to flutter as a bird flew past. There she had discovered an old Shaker table and its ancient owner whose face was as furrowed as his land ever was. She described how this simple man of the soil had conned her into doing his chores as they dickered over the table's price. She knew from experience that the bargaining must appear to be lackadaisical on both sides, so she struggled heroically through the egg collecting and the chicken feeding and the raking of the barn and every so often brought the desultory conversation back around to that old table she thought might be the very thing she needed for displaying her plants on her porch. After nearly three hours of steady labor on her part, and equally intense lounging on his, Enid finally asked him outright to state his price.

He seemed to be mulling the matter over and eventually

announced an astronomical figure from which he would not come down. She huffed at the injustice of the price and the soreness of her back and peremptorily informed him that he must be mad.

He seemed to consider that, too, for some time and then spoke slowly and deliberately. "Well, now. P'raps yer right. I never did care much for that pokey old table there. I could be crazy at that. But—" she thought by the time he finished drawling out the word she'd be his contemporary—"then here you are wanting that table. I've still got it and my morning's work done for me. And, well, next week there's bound to be some other collector of such stuff out here who's willing to do a little summat on the old place while waitin' on me to make up my crazy old mind."

It was a seemingly idyllic family evening. The oldest girl Tom Sawyered her younger sisters into clearing up the dinner things, while she made popcorn and root beer floats all around. Trout remained at table, enjoying the performance as each of his daughters in turn made the kitchen her stage, and only peripherally wondered at Enid's departure as he heard the slap of the screen door and the complaint of the porch rocker.

When everything had been washed, wiped, or swept, Trout and the girls adjourned to the front porch and settled onto the cracked and peeling painted wicker furniture that had graced the front porch of Enid's childhood home. The theatricals continued, punctuated by good-natured jibes and insults until after midnight, though Enid's contributions progressively waned.

The heat had rolled out and the Maine summer night was as crisp as a midwestern autumn evening. It was a night distinguished by no remarkable thing but would be warmly recalled in the close and distant future by the three young women when they thought about family in general or their own in particular.

No one wanted to be first to disturb the closeness. Each feared another would slice through the air with a murmured good night, so they lapsed into stillness.

Wordlessly Trout drew their attention to Francie, the nine-year-old baby of the brood. She had drifted off to sleep in the night quiet and warmth of feeling. Watching her, they recognized the conclusion of the day.

Trout lifted Francie, who remained serenely undisturbed by his unaccustomed efforts. He stood as if hoisting a prize while his two older daughters kissed him on opposite cheeks, embraced their mother, and disappeared into the house. Trout lingered on the porch for a moment, watching Enid's face staring out into the darkness as she sat softly outlined by the light that spilled out from the living room, and he was sated with a sense of well-being such as he had not known for some time.

Deftly he unlatched the door and carried their sleep-heavy child up the stairs and arranged her on her bed. Gently he removed her sneakers, unfastened the thick leather belt with its metal buckle fashioned in the form of a beer logo, and slipped the painstakingly faded and unnecessarily patched jeans off her legs that somehow touched him with their thinness. He turned at the door to survey his handiwork, came back and, stooping, kissed her lightly on the forehead.

As he reached the bottom of the stairs he played with the idea of settling in with Enid and waiting for the sun. He was fairly humming as he came out, but the porch was deserted.

He explored the kitchen and the little library-sitting room off the living room. They were empty, too. When he reached their bedroom he saw Enid's clothes, which characteristically were hung or precisely folded, lying in a hasty little heap on the dresser. She was already in bed, pretending to be asleep.

Trout had a physical sensation of the flood of well-being evaporating even to the drying of his mouth and the parching of his lips. He slept not at all that night.

CHAPTER 5

Looking and feeling as though he had a monumental hangover, Trout was ensconced at his desk the next morning. His
fingers tenderly probed his temples as if reassuring themselves
that all was still intact. He was halfheartedly overseeing the
tidying up of the premises following the departure of the
sundry persons who had interested themselves in the Nathan
Adams case. Agronski and Homer could manage quite well
without his superfluous instructions, and he didn't want to be
there, but he wanted to be away from home even more.

He was aware that he was sulking but he felt entirely
justified in doing so. Enid hadn't spoken a word to him on
getting up and that hadn't happened since the early years of
their marriage. When he finally asked if something was wrong,
she favored him with a long, direct look, appeared insulted and
vanished into the kitchen, shielding herself from further contact
by entering into the chatter of their daughters.

He was angry with her because she made him feel guilty and

he found himself inwardly insisting again that he had nothing to feel guilty about. Yet he knew precisely why she had withdrawn behind a curtain of silence. She felt he had done the same to her.

It had taken him years to understand that for Enid the one unforgivable sin was holding back. Every other transgression, large or small, she could view in the light of extenuating circumstances, but she required a kind of total self-revelation that had been very difficult for Trout to accustom himself to. When they were first married Enid had waited for him to lay his secrets like trophies before her. Then the waiting itself became a silent reproach. In time he had acquired the ability to share his thoughts and had even come to enjoy the comfort he derived from doing so.

Trout was convinced that she knew he had not betrayed her in the classic sense, nontheless she felt betrayed, because she sensed that his feelings about Eve Galatea were to remain private.

He was in the midst of bitterly reflecting that Enid would much prefer him to seduce and confess than to envision a relationship that would never that place, when the phone rang. He signaled to Agronski to take the call in the outer room. Trout was toying with a matchbook and the idea of phoning Eve Galatea when Agronski came softly into his office.

"Miss Galatea has been shot."

"My God," Trout hissed as he lurched up from his chair. He was momentarily transfixed by an image of a hospital room with her lying back against the pillows smiling weakly into his eyes and him willing his strength into hers. "Where is she? How serious is it?" he rapped out, his emotion abrading his voice.

"I'm sorry. She's dead, sir."

Trout stared beyond Agronski, unblinking and unyielding.

"Perhaps, sir, it would be better if I went on to the cottage alone, for photographs, dusting, all that. You might need to stay here to call the medical examiner and, well . . ."

That obvious, thought Trout as he emerged from limbo.

"No, Homer's adept at push-button dialing. We'll go together."

There wasn't much to see except Eve Galatea's body
slumped across the bed like a cloth doll carelessly dropped,
which seemed to convince Trout that she was indeed dead. He
snapped his head away from the body, looking intently at any
and all other contents of the room.

The revolver was there on the floor by the door. A pretty
little thing. It looked more like a piece of jewelry than a
weapon. Agronski suggested that the gun had belonged to a
woman. Trout grunted "maybe" in response and sat woodenly
in a chair across from the bed, head averted, while Agronski
dusted for prints.

The gun had been wiped clean, as had the knobs on the
outside door and the door to the bedroom.

"Except for the gun, our murderer's fastidiousness was
probably unnecessary," Agronski sighed. "That's the trouble
with rented rooms—there are fingerprints on top of fingerprints all over the place. I got a couple sets of clear prints off
the attache case and the cosmetic bottles, but they're identical,
so they must be the victim's."

"Keep at it," Trout snapped as he moved over to the attache
case. That interested him. He had a sudden inspiration that its
contents would explain everything. It's so unlike her, he
thought. His fingers fumbled with the clasps. When he pried it
open he discovered its contents to be tubes of paint, some
brushes, a palette knife, and an assortment of rags. He closed
the case and retreated to the motel to question the owners
about the previous night.

It was a motel and cottage arrangement. Trout knew the
couple who owned and operated it, Norman and Alice Collier.
They were particular friends of Enid. Norman and Enid had
spent many deliriously happy hours together as children, playing doctor, Trout supposed.

Alice claimed Enid as her closest friend. Trout knew that
was insurance against Norman straying in that direction. Enid
didn't reciprocate fully, but neither did she avoid the Colliers.

It was one of those arrangements in which one couple presses close to another, wanting to share holidays and recipes and baby clothes, and the other couple follows the path of least resistance. Trout didn't enjoy the company of either Norman or Alice and he was convinced that Enid felt the same, though she would never admit it, even to herself. She had a unholy reverence for the past, and Norman and Alice Collier were a part of hers.

Alice was waiting for him. She held the screen door open. He passed in wordlessly and sat at the table across from Norman while Alice poured him a cup of coffee.

"Any ideas?" Norman asked.

"Precisely what I was going to ask you."

"It's horrible," Alice said with a shiver. "Therese, the young girl we have this summer to do up the rooms, found her this morning when she went in with her pass key. There was no response to her knock . . ." Alice's voice trailed off.

Trout turned back to Norman. "Did she have any visitors last night?"

"The cottages are actually pretty removed from the motel. And when we're this full you just don't pay any attention to the cars that come and go."

Alice approached with eyes hotter than the coffee in front of him. "It seems unlikely she'd have any night callers. From what I've heard her only friend in town is you."

Trout wondered if that last remark was the product of a heart to heart with Enid or if Alice had seen him with Eve Galatea at the tavern. He bristled under the reproach in her voice. Goddam small town, he thought.

Norman silenced Alice with a look and faced Trout again. He was all commiseration and locker room understanding. He was more irritating than Alice.

"Did you hear the shot or an unexplained noise, a car backfiring?"

"Not that we noticed. We're so close to the coast road that we're accustomed to noises during the summer season. Even at night this stretch of road is fairly heavily traveled. And that cottage is far enough away from everything and everyone else that I guess even a gunshot might go unremarked."

"There is one thing," said Alice with a stiffness that indicated her unwillingness to discuss anything with Trout.

She's another one who'd love to hear my confession, absolve me and tell me to go and sin no more, Trout thought dully. "Well?" He waited.

"The gun on the floor of the bedroom. It belonged to Miss Galatea."

"How do you know?" Trout was beginning to think Alice knew everything. The Rona Barrett of Fells Harbor.

"A few days ago Therese was checking to see if the motel stationery needed replacing and saw the gun in the desk drawer of the living room. She's not a snoop but nevertheless she felt she ought to tell me about it."

"You never said anything," jerked an offended Norman.

"I didn't think it was any of our business," she responded.

Grand, thought Trout. It's nice to know her position on meddling. "Grand," he said aloud.

The medical examiner had fixed the time of death between one and two in the morning. Trout felt a glimmer of relief. He and Enid were in bed then, carefully not touching, staring at opposite walls. At least his whereabouts were accounted for. The way everyone seemed to be regarding him—with a mixture of sympathy and suspicion—he was grateful for an alibi and a hostile witness.

There was no question that it had been murder. George Cox had determined that she had been shot at a distance of about five feet. No signs of a struggle. Apparently nothing stolen. Jewelry, purse, credit cards, money: all intact. Clearly the murderer had been admitted by Eve Galatea unless he, or she, had a key. That seemed unlikely.

And she had been killed by her own gun, which presumably only Therese, Alice and Eve Galatea herself knew the location of. Trout felt grim pleasure at the notion of indicting Alice

Collier for the murder—she had access to the cottage, by her own admission knew where the revolver was kept, and her motive was the avenging of wronged womanhood. Alice might cheerfully kill me, thought Trout, but not Eve. I'll have to find a less dramatic way to remove her from my social circle.

Trout concentrated on regarding the shooting as a case that required solving. He was careful to think of Eve Galatea only as a corpse. He wanted very much to determine who had murdered her, but he told himself that was his job, not his passion.

It struck him that his detachment was so complete as to be peculiar, but he dismissed that from his thoughts as quickly as it surfaced. He was doing a lot of that lately.

Agronski had been uncharacteristically pessimistic about the likelihood of discovering whodunit. As he said, the weapon was hers, there were no witnesses, not even a remotely circumstantial piece of evidence to tie anyone to Eve Galatea. Personal gain on the part of X had to be ruled out—no theft and Agronski had ferreted out the fact that Miss Galatea's estate was left to a small but grateful art museum in New York.

To Agronski had fallen the task of interviewing Therese, the current maid at the Collier motel, though Homer signaled a strong bid in that direction. It seems that in the previous year Therese had reigned as Miss Maine Potato and Homer had secretly desired to bite into her ever since. Agronski was typically unimpressed with her charms and reported that she had no further information.

Reluctantly Trout pushed away from his desk and announced that he could be reached at the Hornsby house. He would be questioning Gretchen Bergstrom. There didn't seem to be anyone else with a motive, and he wanted to talk with her before the shooting was made public.

Trout was careening along the coast road, contemplating a tune-up when he realized he had nearly overshot the mansion. He swerved onto the private road and generously admired the landscaping. He was particularly envious of the day lilies that flanked either side of the drive.

Mrs. Adams herself answered the door. She seemed startled
by his presence.

"I take it Gretchen is not up and around yet?"

"She seems very much better today, actually. A bit remote,
perhaps, but calm and lucid. Was it concern for her that
brought you here?"

Trout could feel the old woman measuring him, tabulating
appearances and intuitions. "Partly. I have to speak with her."

"Today? Is it really necessary?"

"It is."

"I'm afraid I must demand your reasons. She is better, but I
think seeing you could be very disturbing for her now. I have
to consider her welfare and, considering the verdict yesterday,
your request seems unnecessary and ill considered."

"Eve Galatea was murdered early this morning."

"How terrible." She was shaken but as one is on learning of
a distant earthquake or an airplane crash taking anonymous
lives. Her more present concern was the protection of the
young woman struggling with reality in one of the upstairs
rooms. "You can't imagine that Gretchen is responsible for
that," she said, making the obvious leap.

"I don't know," said Trout simply, "but I have to find out.
You can see, can't you, that after her scene at the inquest it's
going to be a widespread conclusion. Look, she has to be
questioned. Better here than in my office. You can refuse. She
can refuse. Then I'll have to take her in. I doubt that she could
handle that."

"Mr. Trout, I like you. I have from that first awful day we
met. But I've heard you speak of Eve Galatea, and I watched
you watching her in that courtroom yesterday," she said
shrewdly. "I don't think either of us can expect you to be
impartial under the circumstances. What assurance do I have
that you will treat Gretchen fairly?"

"I guess none."

"All right," she sighed. "You are probably as honest a man as
I have ever know. I guess I'll have to rely on that."

"If Gretchen did it," he said gently, "it's better for her and you that we find out. She might be a very dangerous young woman."

Mrs. Adams had sketched for Trout the movements of the household on the previous day as far as she knew them. Cutter had come to the house immediately after the inquest to check on Gretchen. He returned to his office for the afternoon. After seeing his last appointment, he came back to the Hornsby house where he had been invited to dine. The day help had left following dinner. Gretchen had remained in her rooms, chiefly in bed. Mrs. Adams had just suggested that Gerald see if he might bring her up a tray when they heard a thud followed by an ominous silence. Apparently Adams and Cutter enacted a Keystone Cops sequence, each attempting to be first to mount the stairs and gain access to the room, bumping and tripping each other the entire journey. Upon entering they discovered Gretchen sprawled across the floor, a pair of manicure scissors lying near her and her left wrist slashed and bleeding.

Fortunately she had fainted—Trout had thought that only happened in horror movies and virgin-versus-villain melodramas, but Gretchen had managed it twice in one day—before having reached an artery. Cutter had patched her up and decided to spend the night in one of the many spare rooms.

When she came to, she was surprisingly calm and grateful that her attempt had not succeeded. She apologized to everyone in turn, and though she evinced embarrassment, offered no explanations. Cutter seemed reassured that there would be no sequel to the last scene, and he retired to bed. Exhausted, Mrs. Adams followed suit, leaving Gerald at Gretchen's bedside, engaged in quiet but earnest conversation.

Mrs. Adams speculated that it must have been around midnight when she heard the door to Gerald's room close. She rose and checked on Gretchen, who was sleeping quite soundly, and then returned to her room to do the same. As for what passed between then and 6 A.M., her regular waking hour, she could not say.

Gretchen was still asleep and remained so through breakfast, which was served at seven-thirty. After breakfast Gerald cloistered himself in the library, where he was still; and Dr. Cutter looked in on Gretchen and then departed for his office with a promise to return this afternoon.

Mrs. Adams concluded her monologue with "It's hardly likely, is it, that in her state Gretchen would have awakened and scurried out into the night to murder Eve Galatea?"

Trout looked at the stately unruffled figured before him and shook his head. "The only thing I can say with assurance is that when it comes to Miss Bergstrom, the unlikely is to be expected."

Mrs. Adams seemed to draw on a hitherto unrevealed supply of hauteur. "Perhaps, Mr. Trout, I misjudged you. I begin to regret my frankness. You seem determined to believe Gretchen a murderess."

"I think Gretchen could be entirely ruthless given the right circumstances, but the details and the timing make her an unlikely candidate.

"I'd also like to speak with your son and with Dr. Cutter when he arrives."

"Of course. May I be present while you question Gretchen?"

"I'm sure that will make it easier for her. I promise to leave my rubber hose downstairs."

"Gretchen, dear, Mr. Trout is here. He wants to talk with you."

"There's no need to treat me like a child, Mrs. Adams," she said, pulling herself up against the headboard of the old four-poster. "Something's happened," she stated, looking from one to the other. "You can tell me. I'll neither scream nor faint. We'll none of us be embarrassed."

"Eve Galatea was murdered early this morning," Trout said.

Gretchen's gaze flew to Mrs. Adams, where it remained fixed while a wealth of emotions traversed her features. She seemed to deliberately choose among them for her reaction, a strange sulking sort of defiance.

"I don't care. Why should I?" Her voice was thin and brittle but gave no sign of breaking.

Mrs. Adams was startled. "Gretchen," she said gently, "you must understand that after the inquest a great many people are going to think you have reason to care."

"You think I did it," she said calmly, turning to Trout. "As they say, that's your problem. Since I didn't, I imagine you won't be able to prove otherwise."

"My job isn't to prove that you did it; it's to find out who did. You happen to be the logical starting place. You know something about Eve Galatea that I don't, and I want you to tell me about it."

"You're mistaken."

"In the courtroom—"

"Utter nonsense. A paranoic outburst. I was not well." She spoke with detachment as though describing a third party.

"And afterwards?"

"What do you mean?" she asked, suddenly wary.

"In your state of semiconsciousness you kept repeating the word 'abomination.'"

"Yesterday the whole world seemed abominable. We all have our off days, Sheriff."

"You apparently had a difficult evening as well," Trout returned, staring pointedly at her bandaged wrist.

"That," she said disparagingly. "That should convince you not to take anything I said yesterday seriously. I was clearly not myself. I'm sure Dr. Cutter could supply you with all the medical terms that apply to my behavior. It was, however, a temporary condition and since I am quite recovered you should not expect me to make sense of it now."

"Can you reconstruct the events of the day?"

"Must I?" she said wearily.

"It would help."

"I remember sitting in the courtroom feeling as though I was actually suffocating. I couldn't breathe; I was sure I was dying. That's when I called out, I guess. After that it becomes difficult. I remember waking in my own bed feeling very angry that I was still alive. So I decided to remedy that, rather ineffectually, I am glad to say. I don't know when I came to

again, but when I did I found everyone around me. They stayed
with me for some time, until, I suppose, they were convinced I
'wouldn't try anything foolish' again. Then Dr. Cutter and
Mrs. Adams left the room. Mr. Adams stayed and talked with
me. He was still sitting by the bed when I fell asleep. I awoke
at ten-thirty this morning. That's it. Now you know as much as
I do."

Trout doubted that.

"Rosebud," she said with a dry laugh.

"Pardon?"

"You remember—in the movie *Citizen Kane*. It opens with
the Orson Welles character who's dying muttering 'rosebud.'
Everyone goes to great lengths to determine the significance of
that one word. It turns out to be nothing more than the name
of the sled he had used as a boy. I hope you enjoy your
investigation, Sheriff."

Mrs. Adams joined Trout in the hallway. "I'm afraid she
isn't as well as I had hoped. I had better stay with her until Dr.
Cutter arrives." She gave Trout directions to the library.

The door was ajar, so he rapped at it softly and went in.
Gerald remained oblivious of his entrance; he was immersed in
pushing papers back and forth across the desk. Trout stood
watching him, wondering again if the taut executive had
always been present inside the flaccid son.

"The door was open," he said finally.

Gerald looked up, startled. "Come in," he said after the fact.
Trout shrugged and Gerald added, "Well, then, sit down."

Trout sat opposite him at the desk and surprised himself by
having to stifle feelings of obsequiousness.

"Did you come to discuss the outcome of the inquest? Very
kind of you, but we were promptly informed of the verdict. I
know you'll understand my relief that it's all over and we can
get back to the business of living, and the business of business."
His glance encompassed the mounds of neatly typed verbiage
between them.

"I wish it were as simple as that. Eve Galatea was killed
early this morning."

"Killed? What do you mean?"

"Shot."

"Robbery? Rape?"

"I wish it had been," Trout said dully. As Gerald's eyes widened, Trout continued. "If it had been a random act of violence, she would be a victim. I hate to think of her as having some complicity in her own death."

"You think this is related to Nathan somehow?"

"I can't think anything else." Trout paused. "I've already spoken with Gretchen."

"No!" Gerald almost shouted. "You can't possibly imagine—"

"Tell me why not."

"You heard what happened here last night?" Trout nodded his affirmation. "Afterwards I sat with her. She had been sleeping for some time when I left."

"What time was that?"

"I don't know."

"Your mother said it was around midnight. She still had enough time."

"She was asleep, I tell you."

"That might have been a ruse or she could have awakened. You were in bed. You have no way of knowing."

"Why? What reason could she have had?"

"She hated Eve Galatea. Even before she ever saw her. Come off it, Gerald; we both know that Gretchen doesn't always need a reason for the things she says or does."

"Gretchen couldn't kill anyone."

"Gretchen is capable of anything." Trout lectured like a tutor to his slow-witted charge. "Look, she loved your brother maniacally, she detested the very idea of Eve Galatea, she fell apart at the sight of her, and she tried to kill herself last night."

"You want it to be Gretchen," Gerald said with sudden loathing. "You want your Eve Galatea to have been senselessly murdered. You're as desperate as Gretchen ever was—"

This tirade was cut off as Gerald's eyes riveted on the open doorway. Trout followed Gerald's gaze to find Dr. Cutter at the end of it. He wondered how long he had been listening.

Dr. Cutter begged their pardon and was about to pass on when Trout asked him to remain.

"Are you finished with me?" Gerald said sullenly.

"For the time being, thank you."

"Then, if you don't mind, I'll go upstairs. I hope, Doctor, you can help Mr. Trout. Perhaps in all your pharmacopoeia you have some antidote for delusions." He closed the door resoundingly behind him.

"Miss Galatea has been murdered," Cutter said quickly so Trout would not have to repeat what he had overheard anyway. "And apparently you think Miss Bergstrom was involved."

"It seems possible," Trout said in his noncommittal professional tone.

"Time of death?"

"Between 1:00 and 2:00 A.M."

"You can eliminate Gretchen."

"So I'm told. Regularly."

"She couldn't have done it."

Trout's attention was focused now. The mantle of weariness he had worn since Gerald's irate departure fell from his shoulders.

"Mr. Adams was still with Miss Bergstrom when I went to my bedroom. That was at about eleven o'clock. I had intended to read for a while, but the books at hand didn't interest me and I fell asleep almost immediately. When I awoke I thought I had just dozed off briefly, but my watch indicated that it was nearly a quarter to two.

"It had been my wish to sedate Miss Bergstrom. I had not done so because she was adamantly against it. She wanted very much to talk with Mr. Adams without nodding off in the middle of a sentence. She had seemed amazingly stable . . . considering. But then I had this mental picture of her lying sleepless—there's something lonely and frightening about sleeplessness even under the best of circumstances. So I made this heroic dash down the hall to rescue her.

"I needn't have. Her sleep was deep and untroubled. Unless you believe in out-of-body travel, I think you'll have to agree it was impossible for Miss Bergstrom to have murdered Miss Galatea from her bed."

"Parry and thrust. You are, I take it, quite sure about the time? You don't need to answer. Your smugness speaks for itself."

"Where do you go from here?"

"I don't know."

"Miss Galatea was from Boston, wasn't she? Maybe the solution is there."

"Maybe."

"You don't look well."

"Expanding your practice? You had better gather the family together and tell them that Gretchen is off the hook. Your popularity is going to rise in direct proportion to the decrease in mine."

CHAPTER 6

I'm home, Enid," Trout called from the door.

The tone of her "hello" added great distance to the journey her greeting made from somewhere in the kitchen.

She was chopping vegetables from the garden: eggplant, zucchini, tomatoes. Ratatouille, he guessed. Either she's working off her knife wielding inclinations or calling a truce. She hates to make ratatouille.

He loved to watch Enid in the kitchen. She claimed that she disliked cooking, but Trout had never believed her. She would wrap herself in the immense white apron, tie it firmly at her waist and roll up her sleeves. He liked it when she smelled of onions and efficiency and had flour on her arms. Something from his childhood, he supposed. He felt a sheepish sort of pride when she would measure out things in handfuls or pinches and concentrate with furrowed brow on the correction of the seasonings. She in turn was always disparaging her results, asserting that anyone could cook, it was only a matter of following a recipe.

Trout didn't want to speak. He didn't want to disturb the rites and benedictions Enid was performing.

It's funny, he thought, how words can never be recaptured. Once spoken they exist by themselves. The speaker can leave, but the words hang on, suspended in the air. For that matter, the speaker can die, but he can't kill the words; they live forever.

Trout was sitting at the table, smoking his third cigarette, when he said, almost casually, "Eve Galatea was murdered this morning." He was tired of saying it.

"Oh!" she said as she dropped the chopping knife, then added more deliberately, "Do you want to tell me about it?"

"Yes." He felt he was surrendering something and it was a great relief.

Enid moved away from the counter, rinsed her hands, and wiped them on the hem of the apron. She poured two glasses of iced tea and sat across the table from him.

"George Cox places the time of death between 1:00 and 2:00 A.M. Whoever did it was given access to the cottage by Eve." He realized that was the first time he had spoken only her given name. Death had reduced her from a personage to a person. "There was no forced entry. She was shot. By a handgun that belonged to her, but there was nothing to indicate a struggle, no reason to believe someone wrestled the gun away from her. It's as though she hired someone off the streets to kill her."

"Could it have been someone she knew from Boston?"

"It's possible. She might have told a score of people that she'd be here and with the press coverage of the inquest her whereabouts weren't exactly top secret. But it doesn't make sense. Why kill her here; why not in Boston?"

"You think it was someone who lives here."

"I thought it was Gretchen. You know, the hysterical secretary. But Dr. Cutter gave me an alibi for her, after I had earned the undying hostility of the residents of the Hornsby house.

"As a matter of fact, I seemed to inspire hostility wherever I went today. I had to talk to Norm and Alice since it was their place she was staying at. For some reason Alice seemed inclined to pour hot coffee on my lap. I was tempted to check the sugar bowl for broken glass." Trout was comforted by Enid's look of puzzlement. He should have known she wouldn't snivel on the shoulder of a righteous friend.

"Anyway, I'm left with no logical suspect."

"What about me? I hated her."

"You never met her."

"The hell I didn't. You brought her home with you every night."

"But I—"

"You know precisely what I mean. Don't insult me by denying the trivial. You know what I can't forgive? Not your thoughts or your desires, transparent as they were. It's the being sick of myself. I've been nauseated with jealousy and fear."

Her eyes were damp and her nose was reddening. He could see that she was trembling slightly. Trout watched the last sliver of ice melt in her untouched drink.

"I guess it's a good thing we both know where the other was last night," he said lightly. But he was troubled. It was only the third time he had ever seen her cry.

The evening had gone quietly enough. A shaky sort of peace descended after the confrontation in the kitchen, which was better than the cold war that had preceded it. They had decided on an all-family excursion to the drive-in movie where *Around the World in Eighty Days* was playing again. David Niven always lifted Enid's spirits.

Trout was fumbling for his keys when the phone rang.

"Hullo?"

"I'm sorry to disturb you at home, sir."

Trout groaned inwardly. "That's all right, Agronski. What is it?"

"Well, sir, as you said, Miss Bergstrom was our only suspect and still would be if it weren't for Dr. Cutter's statement. I have a young woman here at the station with some information that might have some bearing on her alibi. I thought you would like to speak with her yourself, sir."

"Is it really necessary for me to play the dedicated inspector? Damn it, can't it wait until morning?"

"I'm sorry, sir. Yes, it can, sir."

Made to feel his lack of courtesy, not to mention dedication, Trout did his penance. "I'll be there in about twenty minutes."

"Yes, sir."

The four women, all perched on the arms of various pieces of furniture, understood well enough the consequences of the bisected conversation they had overheard. Trout brushed Enid's cheek with his lips and recommended that they enjoy themselves and the movie.

He made good time and arrived at the jail before his self-imposed deadline. Ignoring the speed limit with the red light flashing at the back of the car had improved his mood.

When he entered he found Agronski and a giantess of nineteen sitting in the only illuminated corner and engaged in earnest conversation. Agronski turned as the door swung shut, stood up, and said, "This is Patricia Peterson, sir," with the self-satisfaction of a player who has produced the thirteenth trump.

"Patty," the girl offered with a large gummy smile.

Trout grimaced at the name and at the wad of bubble gum that was in evidence when she spoke.

"Miss Peterson's mother used to look after Dr. Cutter's house."

"Light housekeeping. She used to say light housekeeping and then make a joke about her ship coming in. She'd go in to Ratchet Cove four days a week. Two to Dr. Cutter and two to the Bartons. Dr. Cutter was a tidy man, but that Mrs. Barton didn't clean a dish one day to the next. I told Ma it was slavery what that woman expected with the cleaning *and* taking care of the kids. Slave's wages, too. Ma left off going there toward the end, but she stayed with Dr. Cutter 'til she was too feeble to do the work."

"Mrs. Peterson died three years ago," Agronski interjected.

"I'm sorry," Trout put in perfunctorily.

"No need. I was the child of her late life, she used to say, and she would live 'til I was old enough to tend myself. She was wheezy and wicked tottlish for years. That's another reason I expect she stayed on to Dr. Cutter's; he gave her doctoring and medicines, too. In the end she was took by bronkeel nammonia. With complications," she added proudly.

"Then I moved to town. It was wicked lonesome out where we was. I've been at the Ben Franklin store since. I started at the cash register and now I do accounts and inventory, too. I'm thinking of going to school to be a CPA. I've always been wicked good with numbers. Give two numbers with three places each," she instructed. "Come on," she prodded in a slightly injured tone at Trout's failure to respond.

"763 and 442," Trout obeyed in some bewilderment.

Patty blew a bubble and then as though rendering a computer printout said, "In summing that's 1,205. In times its 337,246. That repeating four made it kinda easy."

"I think she's right," gasped Agronski, still laboring over the figures with pencil and paper.

"I'm not being boastful, mind. I just want you to know I'm speaking true."

"You're quite a remarkable girl, Patty."

"Thank you, sir. It don't do no good to no one to keep your lights under a bushel, Ma said. I expect you'll want to ask me your questions now you got a feel for who I am," she said sagely.

"I expect I would if I knew what questions to ask," Trout said, looking at Agronski.

"Well, sir, with Dr. Cutter living over in the Cove and keeping pretty much to himself, not too much is known about his personal life around here. He doesn't even have many patients from Fells Harbor. So I thought it might be useful to find out if he had a maid or a housekeeper. There is a young woman who cleans for him four mornings a week, but she arrives after he leaves and departs before he returns, so she really couldn't tell me anything. I thought I'd come to a dead end when she mentioned Mrs. Peterson. That led me to Patty here."

"Which takes us where, exactly?"

"Well, sir, when Dr. Cutter had guests for meals Patty's mother did the cooking and serving."

"Fascinating."

Agronski shot him a look of mild reproof. "Most of those meals were shared by Dr. Cutter and Miss Bergstrom."

"Had you expected to discover something of that sort?"

"To be honest, sir, no. I just thought we'd better check up on him a bit as he is her alibi."

"And so you did. While I, on the other hand—who saw him with her and heard him speak of her and in retrospect can plainly see the man's in love—I never gave it a passing thought. If I were you, Agronski, I'd run for sheriff in the next election. If I didn't need the salary, I'd vote for you myself."

Agronski appeared distressed by the turn the conversation had taken, as though Trout's suggestion ran contrary to the natural order of things. He cloaked his discomfiture by turning to Patty and requesting her to repeat what her mother had told her of those dinners.

"Ma wasn't a gossipy sort, but she did have to talk to someone. Anyway, about two years before Ma died Dr. Cutter starts inviting this Miss Bergstrom over to supper wicked regular. Ma'd cook and serve and clean up the kitchen. Courting it was for sure, cause Dr. Cutter would go out in his garden and cut flowers when he had them and fuss over the table. He was having her round about once to the week until the time when he put this little box all wrapped up fancy on her plate. When she came he was all excited and laughing and asked if she wanted it for appetizer or dessert. Ma remembered that especially cause she thought it was real clever. That Miss Bergstrom said she didn't want it at all. That was the last time she came, leastways while Ma was there. Ma said she fairly broke Dr. Cutter's heart. That's all I know for fact."

"How long did this, uh, courtship last?"

"More than a year of Ma making suppers for those two. I don't recall exactly."

"Thanks very much for your help, Patty."

"I'm glad to help. I won't ask why you wanted to know these things, cause it's temptation enough now to go telling about being questioned by the sheriff. Good night now."

Agronski escorted Patty Peterson out the door and returned to where Trout sat drawing circles abstractedly over Agronski's arithmetic. Agronski was feeling well pleased with himself. He had an inductive approach to crime, delighting in the gathering and examination of evidence. There was no other way to put it: he loved data. He balanced Trout, who approached a crime deductively, trying to construct it on a foundation of understanding both the perpetrator and the victim.

After a time Trout looked up and sighed, "It's a wicked lousy case."

Trout phoned Dr. Cutter the next morning, arranging an appointment at his office in the Cove. The drive there gave him the opportunity to sort out his feelings, or what remained of them. He recognized his desire both to do his job effectively and to immerse himself in his family; he wanted order. He pondered the type of person who hungered for excitement. The events and his emotions over the last few days had made him feel raw and too vulnerable. He wanted to anticipate nothing more thrilling than the outcome of the World Series.

The murder had to be solved so that he could give proper consideration to mulching his garden and the American League batting averages, but he was apprehensive of what he might unearth. He liked Cutter. He wanted neither to hate nor to hurt the doctor. And he was beginning to doubt that the discovery of what led to Eve Galatea's death would help him get to sleep at night. More than anything, he shrank from learning more about himself.

Cutter's waiting room was something of a surprise. A worn but heavy rose patterned carpet covered the floor. Seating was provided by two deep and indestructible old leather sofas. The walls were a sort of pale pink—Enid would know the exact word—and their only embellishment was an ancient and soothingly faded quilt hung like a tapestry across the largest expanse. There was a short wooden table piled with puzzles off in one corner surrounded by equally sturdy and stubby wooden chairs.

Reading enthusiasts were offered two options: there were Beatrix Potter's books for the young, and the only magazines available were back issues of *Encounter*, a British publication touching everything from the arts to politics. Most unexpectedly there was a liberal assortment of ashtrays—at least one on each flat surface. Trout hadn't seen a medical facility in years that lacked a no smoking sign like a tombstone riveted to the wall. The characteristic mixture of sterility, efficiency, and doom was noticeably lacking. As the ceiling fan whirred steadily, Trout was reminded of the front room of a comfortable boarding house. It needed only a battered upright piano to complete the ambience. He closed his eyes momentarily, half expecting to be enticed by the smell of baking bread, but the only odor he encountered was a faint waft of rubbing alcohol.

The door to the inner chambers opened, and Cutter's receptionist waddled out followed by a serene young woman with twin boys circa two years old at her heels. The woman was definitively pregnant, and her already present offspring made practical use of her condition by playing a game of push-and-shove around her bulk as she sought to make another appointment.

The receptionist beamed at the boys, then turned her lights on Trout. "Mr. Trout? Dr. Cutter is free now. You go right on in. It's the second door."

Trout shuddered a little as he passed the monument to fecundity. He pulled the outer door behind him.

Cutter was sitting at a desk rapidly drawing hen tracks on the file in front of him.

"Twins again?" Trout asked.

Cutter looked up, puzzling. "Hmm? Oh. No, I think we came across a third heart beat today. Can't be sure though, so I'm scheduling her for ultrasound. My first triplets."

Trout was visibly impressed. "That poor woman. She doesn't look more than twenty-five."

"She'd be delighted. Thirty-four to be exact. She'll be fine. She can handle it. Have you come about Miss Bergstrom?"

"Yes."

"She'll be fine, too. I checked on her early this morning."

"Is she well enough for me to question her again?"

Cutter frowned. "I would say so, but isn't that quite unnecessary? You already know she was in bed when Eve Galatea was murdered."

"No," said Trout spiritlessly, "I know that you said she was in bed."

"I see." Cutter's voice was equally expressionless. "You're saying I lied."

"I think perhaps you did."

"Any particular reason, or is it merely because it's more convenient for you to think so?"

"Damn it, Cutter. Why didn't you tell me you had been in love with her?"

"I see," Cutter said again. "You're wrong there. I still love her. Please don't strain your imagination—I don't expect you to understand. I'm well aware she's not your type. You know, I think we could have been your garden variety happy couple if it hadn't been for Nathan Adams. When he disappeared I thought things might work out after all." He looked away from Trout. "I'd rather you didn't feel sorry for me. Save it for yourself."

"Look," said Trout wearily, "you deliver babies and treat allergies; this is my job. Someone's been murdered and the only person that seems to have any motive, real or imagined, is a young woman who has been given a tidy alibi by her would-be lover. Maybe you didn't check on her during the night. Maybe you did and found an empty bed. Maybe your statement was intended to provide an alibi for yourself. Maybe you murdered Eve Galatea for Gretchen."

"Do you believe that?" There was no indignation in Cutter's tone, only mild curiosity.

"It doesn't matter what I believe," Trout said automatically, then he stopped to consider the question. "I guess I don't believe anything. You could help me if you wanted to. You could tell me what you know."

The hopelessness underlying Trout's words seemed to embarrass Cutter. "I can't help you," he said.

Trout sighed and rose to depart. Cutter's voice trailed sadly after him into the hall: "You ought to find yourself a different job."

Trout stopped at a diner in the Cove for some lunch. It was one of the few eating places in the area that was open year-round. He had a bowl of chili followed by a slab of Boston cream pie that tasted as though it had been whipped up entirely from paper products. He consumed every forkful as a way of postponing his drive to the Hornsby house.

He had to see Gretchen Bergstrom again. He would have liked to attribute his uneasiness to indigestion, but he knew it was the result of his own insistence that she was somehow involved in the murder. Even if her whereabouts could not be adequately accounted for—*if* Cutter was lying—how could she have known about the gun? If she'd gone there to confront Eve, she'd gone empty-handed. And why would Gretchen want to kill her anyway? What had Eve said at the inquest that had triggered the explosion in Gretchen's mind?

Gretchen seemed collected enough when Trout last spoke to her. He supposed that could be a kind of insanity, too. Yet he couldn't believe that she was crazy—a bit grim perhaps, from being too much in touch with reality.

When he arrived at the house he found her out on the grounds alone. He was pleased to take that as an index of her improvement, and he was delighted not to have to storm the protective barriers Mrs. Adams and Gerald would undoubtedly have erected.

She was dressed in jeans with a plaid cotton short-sleeved shirt. For the first time Trout saw her as a young woman rather than as a functional being who could type x words a minute. She was kneeling on the ground inspecting toadstools and selecting specimens to place in the woven basket at her elbow.

She didn't look up as he approached but said quietly and without rancor, "I was expecting you earlier. I thought you would come directly from Dr. Cutter's."

"He called you." It was more of a statement than a question.

"Of course." She bent back down to her task. "I'm not gathering these for any sinister purpose," she said lightly. "Have you ever seen a print made with mushrooms? No," she answered herself as if considering his interests and limitations, "why should you have? It's simple really. You take a freshly picked toadstool, lay it on colored paper, leave it until it has dropped its spores and the result is a unique and exquisite print. I imagine it's the symmetry that makes them so fascinating, like with snowflakes and spider webs. I'm hoping to frame some of this batch for Dr. Cutter's office."

"I'd like to see them when you're finished."

"Perhaps you shall."

"Did Dr. Cutter tell you what we discussed?"

"My impression was that it was more of an accusation than a discussion."

"I don't think that's quite accurate."

"Really?" she asked, wearing a mask of incredulity. "And I thought you had crawled through our private lives and emerged with the earthshaking knowledge that Dr. Cutter had once been fond of me and, based on that, assumed that he had either been covering for me about the other night or out committing murder himself. I'm beginning to understand you, I think. You're rather a worm." She finished calmly, as thought offering a conjecture about the weather or some other matter of inconsequence.

"He should have told me about your relationship."

"For God's sake, why? It was a long time ago, and even then there wasn't much to tell."

"I have to wonder if he's telling the whole truth now."

"You're such a fool. Dr. Cutter couldn't kill anyone and I didn't kill anyone."

"But then why won't you tell me what you know about Eve Galatea?"

"You told the coroner that I didn't know anything about her. Dr. Cutter said you were most emphatic."

"That was before she was killed."

"I don't understand what has changed."

"She's dead, damn it."

"How does that change the past?"

"It changes everything."

"What do you expect to learn from me?"

"Who she was."

"You expect a lot. You're the sheriff of this county. You have access to all sorts of information. I'm sure you've found out everything there is to know."

"I haven't found out anything I need to know, the things that you could tell me. I think you knew her, under a different name or maybe years ago."

She laughed with unexpected delight as at the punchline of a suddenly remembered joke. "We were sisters—I'd nearly forgotten. Oh, you don't believe me," she said archly. "Are we more unlikely siblings than Nathan and Gerald Adams?" She laughed again, then shook her head at his evident lack of humor.

"You won't help me, then?"

"I said before that you were a fool. I'd like to take the barb off that: it was only the recognition of a kindred spirit." With that she picked up her basket and headed back toward the house. Trout started to follow, changed his mind in midstep and swung round to his car.

Trout drove along the coast road until he came to a stripe of beach that hemmed the highway but was hidden from view by a ribbon of trees. He needed some time to think away from the dull yammering of Homer and the bright determination of Agronski. He pulled the car into a gap between the trees, removed his shoes and socks, and deposited his feet in the cool chaste sand. He strode the length of the beach twice, then, squinting, determined the middle of the stretch and, returning to it, dropped leaden and immobile except for his burrowing toes.

He knew that behind murder, unlike leukemia or earthquakes, you can always find a reason. As he got older he had come to believe that there was never a good reason, but the point was that the murderer invariably found a compelling enough motivation. Even the visibly unbalanced—the sniper or child abuser, say—had reasons, whether or not those reasons made sense to anybody else.

When you could rule out the two customary inducements for killing—a family dispute or personal gain—you had to start looking for a twisted reason, the product of a bent mind. That's why he kept coming back to Gretchen Bergstrom.

She had had, he assumed, what was usually characterized as a psychotic breakdown. These periodic or even once-in-a-lifetime cataclysmic disintegrations of a personality were not so very uncommon, he knew. His roommate in college had experienced one following a season of seemingly mild depression and then been as right as rain and as fit as a fiddle three weeks later. In different epochs people were treated for hysteria or nerves or melacholia or demonic possession depending upon the perspective of the time. Strange behavior was tolerated and attributed to eccentricity or one's liver or the effects of the full moon. The brain was a surprisingly efficient machine, but there had always been and would always be temporary malfunctions. The only thing that changed was the label we applied to them.

Gretchen's paranoia, her collapse, and the subsequent suicide attempt seemed to fit neatly into the framework of this type of short-lived mechanical failure. What he wanted to know was the role Eve Galatea played in it.

Was the connection simply a coincidence of timing—Eve being just a handy hook to hang her obsessions and prepossessions on? Was she a symbol to Gretchen? Or was she an enemy responsible for some horror that lurked in the secretary's mind?

Trout found he was making about as much progress as the child who endeavors to read from right to left. Struggling with his perceptions of Gretchen's conceptions wasn't going to illuminate the puzzle of who actually killed Eve.

He had to take the enigma of Eve herself as his starting point. He had data—dates and place names, account numbers and pieces of identification. And he had his own impressions to fall back on, but even these were somehow linear. He had hoped, at one time, to have the opportunity to fill in the dimensions.

Of one thing he was absolutely certain: she was unforgettable. And that was the strangest element in this entirely strange case. No one had claimed the body. No one was interested in even discovering the details of her funeral arrangements. The lone inquiry his office received came from her Boston lawyer after Agronski had ferreted him out to determine the disposition of her estate. The murder had made a wire service story and received national coverage because of her recent association with the Adams embezzlement and suicide and because she was an attractive woman, and newspapers are like that. Nearly forty-eight hours had passed and Trout had to conclude that she had no mourners. He found that as unbelievable and irrefutable as the first Apollo moon landing.

As the drowning sun offered a last glimpse of pastel splashes over the greying water, Trout resolved that he would fly down to Boston in the morning.

He made a detour to his office on the way home.

The outer room was veiled in dusk and looked abandoned, but there was a fan of light spilling out the half open door to his private cubicle. His footsteps pounded hollowly across the bare tiles, so Homer had enough warning to rewrap the remains of his ham salad sandwich and remove his feet from Trout's desk. He had at least the grace to look sheepish. He held his breath momentarily, waiting to see if Trout was going to chew him out. When the older man chose to ignore the infraction of rank, he adjusted his mouth to his customary sardonic grin.

Damn kid, thought Trout, even manages to give the impression of swaggering while sitting down.

"Agronski?" asked Trout.

"Went home about a half hour ago. I've been handling things."

I'll bet you have, Trout thought with the glint in his eye matching the gleam in Homer's. I'll bet you've handled every damn thing in my desk.

"Anything come up?"

"Nah, just routine."

Trout was growing impatient and he let it show.

"There was a call for you from the medical examiner, whatshisname Cox," Homer amended quickly.

"Urgent?"

"Nah. He didn't say so, anyway."

"About Eve Galatea?"

"I dunno."

"Maybe there's been a more recent homicide that's slipped your mind?"

"Gimme a break, boss."

Trout hated being addressed as "boss" even more than he did "sir."

"Was there any message?"

"Nah. Just that he called."

Trout motioned Homer out of the door with the receiver he held in his left hand while with his right he flipped the pages of an old desk calendar that served as his phone and address book. His fingers halted at the name of George Cox. He was sweeping Homer's crumbs off his blotter and into a dark green metal wastebasket as the fifth ring was cut off by a slightly breathless but hearty "hello."

"Hello, Sophie. This is Trout. George called a while back, and I thought I'd have a better chance of catching him at home about now."

"It's good to hear from you, Sheriff, even if it is business. You've missed George, though. He left this afternoon for Bangor. I've got the number where he's staying if you want to reach him there."

Trout considered this, then asked, "Do you know what the trip was about, Sophie?"

He could visualize the smiling folds around her eyes as she replied, "Is this your way of telling me I've got competition?"

"George wouldn't risk losing a good thing. Besides, the state of Maine isn't big enough to produce another woman who could be considered competition for you."

"Well," she said, accepting his estimation of her worth, "you know—no fool like an old fool."

"George may be getting older—everyone does but you—but he could never be that big a fool."

"I always have liked you, Sheriff. Now I'm appreciating my own good judgment. George is consulting with a doctor in Bangor."

"Something to do with the Eve Galatea murder?"

"He didn't give me any details. He seemed mighty puzzled about something, though. Sorry I can't be of more help."

"Did he say how long he'd be gone?"

"A couple days. He's going to see this doctor tomorrow. He didn't mention the name or maybe he did and my mind was wandering. But he won't come back 'til the following day. His night driving is a bit shaky these days. He won't admit to that, but I don't say anything because he at least has the sense to avoid driving after dark."

"Unless I reach him tonight I probably won't be speaking with him until the day after tomorrow. I'm going out of state for the day myself."

"Now that's what I call too bad. Your timing's off. George doesn't go out of town very often and hardly ever without me. This could be our only chance."

"Don't tempt me, Sophie. No clandestine affair for us. When you're ready to leave George I'll be waiting. It's got to be all or nothing."

"You and Humphrey Bogart."

"Huh?"

"The only men I know of who can make rejecting a lady seem like the highest compliment."

"I am pleased. I'm sure you're the first woman I've courted to find in me any resemblance to Bogart."

"You just aren't appreciated. Which brings to mind Enid. Are you all coming over for our Labor Day picnic?"

"As far as I know."

"Good. I'll make a point of praising you to your wife. Then she won't suspect I've got designs on you. Give her my love."

Trout copied down the Bangor number she dictated and after one last exchange bordering on the ribald wished Sophie a good night.

Trout had always been fond of Sophie Cox. She had been his teacher in the third grade, but she had the unusual gift of being able to accept former pupils as adults when they came of age.

Her marriage to George was one of those celebrated mismatches that is given about as much chance of success as a coupling in a Thomas Hardy novel but which turns out to be a rare and deep bond despite the predictions and wary watchfulness of friends and family.

George was a conservative and taciturn man; he took everything seriously. In his undergraduate days he had played college football and the determination he displayed on the field earned him the onerous appellation "Fighting Cox." In medical school he maintained his grim demeanor as scrupulously as a cadet tends his full dress uniform. He was the butt of less than tasteful amusements centering around cadavers and skeletal remains. Consequently, when he became interested in forensic medicine, it was almost as though he had carried the joke too far.

Back in Fells Harbor Sophie waited patiently for him to finish college, then for him to finish medical school and his internship and then for him to complete his tour of duty during World War II. They had been engaged since she was in high school, but George didn't want to marry until he had completed his education, and he refused to consider a marriage that might leave his bride a war widow. So Sophie waited.

She had been everyone's ideal high school sweetheart, and her protracted engagement did not deter the bulk of young males who crossed her path from trying to walk by her side. She probably received more proposals than any other woman in Fells Harbor history, thought Trout, not including those of the legions of prepubescent boys she had encountered in her forty-year teaching career. But she was steadfast to the wonder of everyone but George; he had expected no less.

As the years slunk inexorably by, George remained a conscientious technician, a loyal Republican and a man who would never be caught with his collar button unfastened. And, happily, Sophie had remained Sophie, with her wildflowering warmth and affection, somehow gathering more and more people to her without ever seeming to spread herself thin.

The Coxes weren't young any more—there were wags who insisted George never had been, and there were some who pointedly introduced his name into conversations about retirement.

They were perhaps constitutionally ill suited to find happiness in each other.

Trout found them an enviable couple.

He tried the Bangor number without success. It wasn't like George to go off in the middle of a case. At the least Trout would have expected an outline neatly typed in triplicate detailing his reasons for departure and his conclusions, however obvious, thus far. He had to believe the consultation was connected with the shooting; Cox was too methodical and single-minded for it to be otherwise.

He flicked off the light in his office and pulled the door shut behind him. He stopped at the table where Homer sat fish-mouthing perfect doughnuts of smoke into the air. "When you see Agronski in the morning tell him I've gone to Boston for the day."

"A boondoggle, eh, boss?" Homer suggested slyly, reaching for a nonexistent cameraderie. He withered visibly under Trout's stare and choked on his unborn smoke ring. Trout wordlessly left the building.

As he eased himself behind the wheel of the Alfa his attention was snapped back to the structure with its meager offices and cramped cells. He thought, not for the first time, that its rooms were interchangeable. He sighed as he realized that what had drawn his gaze back was the sudden rectangle of light confined by his office window.

"You're late," Enid said without reproach.

Trout knew that no apology was expected, that Enid was asking if it was proper to inquire the reasons in front of the girls.

"I got tied up." He accepted the can of beer she took from the refrigerator. "I have to make a trip down to Boston tomorrow to see Eve Galatea's attorney." The announcement was for the children. The discussion was postponed.

The girls expressed mild curiosity, which was satisfied easily, and then turned the conversation to more pressing concerns: the approaching end of summer, the impending doom of another school year, wardrobes that were shamefully passe and the tragedy of Jenny Atwood's boyfriend returning to New York with his family.

As though readying themselves for the routine of autumn, all three girls went to bed early, leaving a mixture of anticipation and regret in the air.

Though Trout had been out of school for many years and had neither the intention nor the least desire to return, he didn't have to rely on memory to experience the sweet-sour tang that flavored fall. His birthday fell in March, but the years were measured off with each successive Labor Day. That was when he aged; that was when he took stock and made his new year's resolutions.

Enid dealt with her nostalgia, her awareness of the passing of time made suddenly acute, in a different way. While Trout took long rambling walks or sat unreading with a book in his hands, she was a flurry of activity. She vigorously baked and cleaned, tasks that normally held no appeal for her. She even put up jars from the summer harvest. She shopped and scurried, mended and mothered and polished, and prepared for the icy fingers and snowy feet of winter.

"I nest and you brood," she said aloud, summing up his thoughts. She was smiling at him and at the myriad of plans and projects that would overfill the coming days.

"What are you knitting?"

"A sweater for Sophie. You inspired me with your talk of her this evening. I haven't been to see her for months now."

"Damn. I wonder what made George bustle off like that. Better try calling him again." Trout dialed the number Sophie had given him, waited eight rings, then replaced the receiver roughly.

"What do you expect to find in Boston?" Enid asked finally.

"I wish I knew. I want to get more of a feel for her." He

could see the caustic rejoinder forming on Enid's lips, so he hastened on; "I know when she was born and where, her parents' names and the dates of their deaths, when she moved to Boston, and not much in between. I could take the FBI report and the information I got from her in conversation, and the combined data wouldn't begin to cover an index card. There has to be more."

"How will it help?"

"I have to try to understand why she was killed before I can arrive at who did it. Why someone hated, or maybe loved, her that much."

"You've ruled out the secretary?"

"No. I haven't ruled out anyone. As long as I see no reason for the murder, she'll be my only suspect."

"You hope to clear her?"

"Yes." Trout paused and then produced "No" with a violence that surprised even himself.

CHAPTER 7

There was a landing field for light aircraft about twelve miles inland from Fells Harbor. Naturally none of the big commercial lines used the field. It had been established during World War II as part of the effort to Protect Our Coast. A couple of planes were used to transport freight, a few were leased by local guides to hunting and fishing parties and for flying lessons, and the remainder were privately owned by those familes who could still afford their leisure homes but couldn't afford to renounce business altogether. Trout had made arrangements to travel aboard a freight craft. He cursed himself and his budget, for anything smaller than a DC-10 induced in him thoughts of the disposition of his meager estate and a nagging nausea.

He was acquainted with his pilot, a sky cowboy named Hank Giroux, a member of one of the myriad French Canadian families that had filtered down into Maine over the centuries, making the northern reaches of the state as bilingual as the southern stretches of Texas.

"I'll be taking off from Logan at about seven this evening. I'll check with the tower when we land, but that's the tentative schedule. If you're not there, I'll assume you've made other arrangements."

"Yeah. I'll be there," Trout said between clenched teeth. "You know you don't have to do anything fancy to impress me, just stay aloft and preferably in the same position."

Giroux chuckled—in French, of course—and offered to turn the controls over to Trout. Trout blanched but made no response. Conversation was difficult as all of Trout's energy was focused on willing the plane to remain horizontal and forbidding his stomach to make a vertical flight.

"What are we carrying?" Trout asked in the hope of inspiring a monologue that might distract him from his preoccupation with the heavens and the heaves.

"Mostly lobster," came the unelaborate reply.

Trout glanced down at the sunlit waters, which he saw transformed into an ocean of melted butter.

"Damn you," snapped Giroux, noting the rapid rise and fall of Trout's Adam's apple. "There's a bag under your seat. Get it and be quick."

Trout rinsed out his mouth repeatedly at a sink in an airport restroom. Then he vigorously washed his face and scrubbed his hands and deplored the ubiquitousness of brown paper toweling. After realigning his tie and purchasing a roll of peppermint Lifesavers, he felt ready to delve into the affairs of Eve Galatea.

Sitting in the taxi, which he knew to be an extravagance considering the distance he must cover, he thought again of the peculiarity of the location of the office of Eve Galatea's attorney. The address wasn't downtown; it wasn't even in Boston. It was a Mass. Ave. number which, according to the first two digits, must be situated in Arlington, if memory served.

Arlington was a near suburb but not at all suburban. Working and middle class, with ethnic pockets filled with Italians, Irish, Greeks, and Orientals as well. The black population was either nonexistent or invisible. It was very like many neighborhoods in the older and bigger cities and very unlike the sort of place one would expect Eve Galatea's lawyer to locate.

The cab deposited him outside a storefront that declared Edward J. Flaherty in chipped gilt lettering and Paul M. Flaherty in shiny gold letters that looked almost garish sandwiched between the worn top line and the equally aged "Attorney at Law." Trout noted the economy in retaining the singular as he pushed open the door.

The window was a showcase for a cluster of thirsting plants, all sansevieria—probably chosen for their ability to grow without nurturing, or perhaps they were simply the only survivors of a regime of neglect—and an assortment of posters supporting local fund-raising events. The floor was carpeted in a drab olive green that reminded Trout of nothing so much as an army blanket and had about as much nap to it as well. The walls were covered entirely by a lusterless cheap paneling of the kind that seemed to generate spontaneously in middle-class homes during the fifties.

It was a dull unimaginative room that provided the perfect setting for the young man seated behind one of the three desks. The office was otherwise empty.

"Hi, how are ya?" This was said as one word while his arm shot out as though propelled from the elbow. Trout accepted the extended hand and groaned inwardly as the voice boomed, "What can I do for ya?"

"You're Paul Flaherty?"

"Yessir."

Trout extricated his hand from the pumping grasp and announced, "Trout. Sheriff of Halesport County. Maine," he added in response to the dim look.

Flaherty's face registered regret at the loss of the income he'd been calculating and Trout peered closely at the new lines revealed around his eyes and mouth. He had taken Flaherty for a neophyte in his mid-twenties. He was baby-faced with a hank of unruly hair that kept unfurling across his forehead, but scrutiny revealed him to be more than ten years older than first assumed. He had shoulders too broad for his off-the-rack suit.

Trout concluded from this and his hearty hale-fellow manner
that he was and ever would be a jock, not of the tennis/hand-
ball breed but the street hockey with the guys from high school
type who would always be his closest friends despite the level
of their communication, which relied heavily on formulae and
grunts.

"Yessir, what can I do for ya?"

"Did you handle Eve Galatea's affairs?"

Flaherty permitted himself a lecherous grin. "Who else? The
old man hardly ever even comes in any more, uh . . ." He was
searching his memory for Trout's first name and not finding it
put him off balance. He was one of those naturally political
animals who dropped all commas and periods from his speech
and instead punctuated each sentence with the first name of his
listener. "You see, uh . . . he really can't cut it anymore. I keep
telling him he ought to retire, but it makes him feel big in the
neighborhood. You know how it is, uh . . ."

Trout said he knew how it was, but brusquely, trying to
stifle these efforts at cameraderie, which he knew would grow
increasingly annoying.

"How did Miss Galatea come to you?"

"In a cab." He was visibly pleased with his prompt wit. "I
asked her who recommended me. I was curious to know if
anybody I knew knew anybody like her." He paused to give
Trout time to sort this out. "She said she got my name from the
newspaper, uh . . . We can advertise now, you know. We have
this little ad that we run in *The Herald American* once in a while.
My wife designed it—it's very dignified."

"What matters did you handle for Miss Galatea?" Trout
steered hard away from the subject of Flaherty's wife, expecting it to be followed by either children or in-laws.

"Just the will. It's funny. She had a sizable estate to dispose
of. More than you and I will ever see." Flaherty might have
winked to confirm their rapport. "But then," growing confidential, "I don't expect to make my money from my law
practice, uh . . ." Trout was relieved to hear it. "I'm investing
in real estate. I own three two-families already and I've got a

bid in for this property right here, which is part of a package that runs all the way to the corner. Rental property is the thing." Flaherty tapped the triangular desk-top NOTARY sign with his index finger. "This has been my best investment. You wouldn't believe how much valuable information comes my way—about who's selling and what's available—just through people who come in to get things notarized." He leaned far back into his chair with his arms winged out and his hands folded above a burgeoning pot belly. In that position he brought to mind an overage Peter Pan. Trout waited a half minute to see if the cock would crow.

"What was funny?"

"Huh? Oh, yeah. Like I said, there was a lot of money, but it was all money. Bank accounts, ya know. You and I both know," this time he did wink, "that people with money don't leave it in a bank. If anything they are the ones who are always tapping for a loan—their cash is tied up. You don't get rich by collecting interest."

"You get rich by collecting rent."

"Right!" Flaherty beamed as a teacher at an apt pupil. "She didn't have property or stocks or securities. And I asked her who'd been handling her legal affairs before. You know, uh, how women are. I figured she probably had investments that she didn't know about or maybe had forgotten. But she said she never had a lawyer before. Can you imagine that? Anyway, she was weird."

"In what way?"

"I dunno," he said with rising color as an uncomfortable memory crept over him.

"You made a pass," Trout stated decisively.

"Not a pass. Hell, I knew she was out of my league. I just offered to take her to lunch. To Anthony's on the pier, too." He was hurt that his extravagance hadn't been properly appreciated. "Lawyers do that kind of thing with clients all the time." Now he was pleading his case. "The way she reacted you'd have thought I was scum. And then I was afraid she was gonna take her business elsewhere, so I had to really kiss ass. I mean, that will could have been the start of a very profitable relationship." Trout could imagine the terrible internal struggle that took place between Flaherty's hairy ego and his bald greed. "If I'd known she was gonna die soon, I would have told the bitch just what she could do with her lousy will."

Trout rose abruptly and departed the office, leaving a bewildered Flaherty behind. It wasn't simply that he despised the creature, though he did, but he was very much afraid that in exchanging even the most curt of farewells Flaherty would automatically pat Trout's fanny in adieu, one good sport to another. Trout did not want to punch him.

Why did Eve Galatea want a stupid lawyer? Clearly that's what she wanted, for Trout knew instinctively that she never would have settled for less—or in this case, more—than she required. He fruitlessly pondered this new enigma throughout the cab ride to her apartment house.

The taxi took him into the U-shaped drive and deposited him under the brick and concrete carport thrust well out from the building to shield its important residents from rudely inclement weather. The front entrance was locked with an etched metal plate to one side instructing callers to press the encased button if the security guard was not in view. That gesture was unnecessary, for on this occasion a uniformed man was already striding toward the door. Despite the obvious fact that the guard was on the far side of fifty, Trout judged by his bearing that he was well suited for his job.

"May I help you, sir?" buzzed the grilled box over the door.

Trout was slightly in awe of people who used "may" where most mere mortals slid carelessly into "can."

Trout listed his credentials and then produced verifying identification in response to the guard's polite but firm request. He was given admittance and had to check the feeling of gratitude that was rising in him.

"I'd like to ask you some questions about a former tenant. Is this a good time?"

"May I see your identification again?" Trout handed over his card, which was given close scrutiny. "I'm not giving you a hard time, Sheriff," he said at last, apparently satisfied, "I just want to know who it is I'm talking to. I've been handed phony ID's before, and I'm not about to give information to a private gumshoe.

"The way I see my job is that I'm here to protect the residents. And not just from break-ins. I do a good job. When there's a reason I'm ready to cooperate with the police. You ask your questions and I'll answer *if* I can."

Trout understood the man's emphasis. "I'm here about Eve Galatea."

The man's eyebrows shot up, rearranging the stolid features. "You said '*former* tenant.'"

"She's been murdered."

The large head shook slowly from side to side. It registered no shock, but perhaps dismay at the wicked ways of the world or the vulnerability of one of his wards. "What can I tell you?"

"Let's start with your name."

"Harry Mueller."

"How long have you worked here?"

"Twelve years. Used to be a longshoreman." He was still shaking his massive head. "Anyway, I've been here since before Miss Galatea moved in."

"You were questioned by the FBI a couple weeks ago?"

He nodded. "The guy fed me a line about national security and some position she'd applied for. But I know they're not going to use a security guard as a source for that kind of information.

"The fed wasn't very bright. Rather, I suppose he didn't think I was very bright. He asked me an armload of questions about her callers and then threw in a couple about 'political discussions we might have had' and my awareness of any possible involvement with drugs. As if I'd know. As if I'd think that's what he wanted to know."

Trout thought for a minute that Harry Mueller was going to spit out of the side of his mouth to punctuate his disgust.

"I answered his questions even though I knew he was lying, because I judged I really didn't know anything that could hurt her anyway. I told him she had no callers. As far as I know that's the truth. What was that all about, anyway? Or can't you tell me for reasons of national security?" The disdain had crept back into his voice.

"Don't you read the papers?"

"Matter of fact, I don't. Waste of time." Mueller paused and when he spoke again his voice was rough and unused as on waking. "I used to get angry or excited about facts. Saw information as a weapon for change—you know what I mean. It took me a long time to realize that one man's liberator is another man's terrorist."

Mueller was ponderously articulating his chosen philosophy. As he groped for words to express the thoughts that were still incomplete, Trout understood that these weren't oft repeated time-polished sentiments. Mueller was making a virgin attempt to lay out his ideas for another person's viewing.

"It was the manipulation I resented," he resumed. "One day I was sitting at my kitchen table. I had the *New York Times*, *The Daily Worker*, and *The National Observer* spread out in front of me. It wasn't an experiment or anything. I used to spend my weekends that way—when I wasn't at a meeting or a lecture. I was hungry for information. I wanted to understand," he trailed off.

"Understand what?" Trout pushed gently.

"Hmm? Oh, the truth. It makes men free, you know." The large face opened to let out an unexpected hearty laugh. "Something snapped that day. I guess I just couldn't find any facts. A whole lot of convictions, though. So I chucked my job and took this one. I'm making up for lost time. Here, I'll show you."

Trout followed him around a bay of elevators and into an alcove fitted out with a wooden desk and companion straight-backed chair. The wall behind was lined with books. All fiction and, as far as Trout could tell, none of it current.

"There are no facts here," Mueller said with a sweeping gesture, "but I console myself with occasional glimmerings of truth." He excused himself and brought around one of the padded waiting chairs from the lobby, into which Trout settled comfortably. Trout found himself liking Mueller very much. The guard opened a desk drawer and produced from it a neatly boxed lunch, which he insisted upon sharing. The repast was sporadically interrupted by the flashing of a red button on the light panel of the desk phone. Mueller would then leave briefly to attend to a visitor, a delivery, or a resident who had mislaid a key.

He assured Trout that within the limits of his knowledge Miss Galatea had never received a visitor in her apartment, and he had never seen her leave in the company of anyone. Yes, it had struck him as unusual, but that was all. He was not much given to reflections on the personal lives of the tenants. Mueller and Miss Galatea had exchanged few words and no conversation. Their lengthiest dialogues occurred on those few occasions when he hailed a cab for her. No, he really didn't have any impressions to offer, except that once in his absence Miss Galatea had apparently borrowed a book from his shelves. She left a note and a few days later the book had been returned, also in his absence. No, he couldn't recall which book. Was it important? Then, at Christmas, when most tenants gifted him with an envelope of greenery, he found a brown paper parcel on his desk with "from Eve Galatea" scrawled across it. It was a beautifully bound book and was solely responsible for his inability to purchase paperbacks anymore. Of course, he'd like Trout to look at it.

Trout held the heavy volume in both hands. It was encased in rich green textured leather with its face blank. He turned its spine up so that he could read the title: *Portrait of a Lady*. Trout felt he had come full circle without knowing where he'd started.

Trout tried the door of the manager's apartment with no luck. He decided to have a go at Eve Galatea's immediate neighbors.

Each floor housed three apartments, except for the ground level, which contained the lobby, Mueller's hideaway, and the manager's rooms. He stopped the elevator at the third floor and rapped on the door of 301. He was on the verge of knocking again, when the door opened an inch and a watery blue eye examined him sternly from above the chain.

"Yes?" the voice crackled. "What do you want?" Trout couldn't tell if it was irritation or trepidation that rasped the voice. Then he concluded it was probably neither, merely disuse.

"I'd like to speak with you about your neighbor Eve Galatea. I'm the sheriff of Halesport County, Maine." He turned his identification over to the fingers tipped with startling pink polish extended through the widened crack in the doorway. The hand and eye disappeared for a time, followed eventually by the sound of the chain being unsecured. When the door swung open, Trout confronted an elderly woman of indeterminate age, festooned with jewelry and a slight bluish tinge to her hair. She wore a blue print silky-looking dress with three-quarter-length sleeves, the better to display her bracelets and watch. Her ample bosom supported a brooch of blue stones, and the lobes of her ears were distended by the habitual wearing of heavy earrings such as the ones she now wore.

"Mueller didn't announce you," she said accusingly.

"Sorry. I guess I didn't tell him I was on my way up."

"Well, come in."

"Thank you," Trout glanced down at his notes, "Mrs. Lancaster."

"You're the second one to come asking questions about that woman." She waited for Trout's reaction.

"You mean the FBI agent?"

Mrs. Lancaster was clearly disappointed, as though Trout had overtrumped her trick. "If you know all about that, what are you here for? I don't have anything else to add to what I told him."

"Miss Galatea's been murdered." Trout immediately regretted, considering Mrs. Lancaster's age, that he hadn't softened the announcement. His concern was proven unnecessary.

"What's that got to do with me?" she asked unflinchingly.

She fairly jingled and clanked as she settled herself onto a chair and gestured for Trout to take the one opposite her.

"Nothing, I'm sure. I was just hoping you could tell me a bit about her. Your impressions of her."

"There's nothing to tell. She was a cold fish, that one. I keep to myself and am quite content when others do likewise, but I do expect a little neighborliness. No man is an island, you know."

"Miss Galatea was unneighborly?" Trout prodded.

"Not long after she moved in my phone went dead. This new equipment is so flimsy," quite confidential now, as she warmed to her subject. "So I went over and asked if I could place a call from her phone. Well, before she answered the door she turned off all the lights in her apartment. Pretended she'd been napping. Nobody naps at seven o'clock. Besides, I had seen the light under her door. She wasn't fooling me—she just didn't want to have to invite me to sit a bit. Not many people would go to those lengths to avoid offering an old woman a cup of tea.

"She never did turn the lights on and it was so dim in there I bruised my leg against a table," Mrs. Lancaster rubbed her shin reminiscently. "She yawned from across the room during my entire phone conversation. You can't imagine how insulting it was.

"That's the only time I ever spoke with her. If I want to be pushed around I can take public transportation, but I expect a little respect and courtesy from the people who live here. I pay my rent the same as everybody else, and it's not cheap, mind you.

"You'd think that woman was born fully clothed instead of naked like the rest of us."

Trout savored the picture of this bedizened biddy who despised the users of mass transit and resented a pose of social superiority with equal, if oddly expressed, indignation huffing and fretting each time she met Eve Galatea at the elevator.

He thanked her for her cooperation and bid her good day when she caught his sleeve at the door.

"Where are you going now?" she demanded.

"Apartment 303."

"Mrs. Dorris works during the day. There is no Mr. Dorris. Divorced, *she* says. That's as may be. I just know I've never seen any father coming to visit the boy."

Trout made no response.

"You need to know how reliable your witnesses are, don't you?" Mrs. Lancaster said with rising color. "Well, I suspect that one is no better than she should be."

Trout thanked her again, this time rather brusquely, and turned away from the door, which slammed in the wake of his retreat. He heard the chain lock being fastened behind him. He knocked on the door of 303. This one had a peephole.

"Who is it, please?" came a youngish female voice from the interior.

Trout identified himself and held his card up to the peephole. His distaste for city living was rapidly reawakening. All this concern for security, the remoteness of people who live within a few feet of each other. He felt the smallest twinge of sympathy for Mrs. Lancaster.

"Have you ever had chicken pox?" the disembodied voice called out.

"Yes," Trout responded to this surefire attention getter.

The door opened and the young woman smiled, "I guess it's all right, then."

Before Trout entered he turned his head to find the door at the end of the hall slightly ajar with an eye squinting over the chain lock. The door closed so swiftly and soundlessly that Trout wondered if perhaps he'd imagined it being open.

The television was on in the living room, and there was a boy of about five lying on the couch keeping one eye on the program and the other on Trout, undecided as to which would prove more interesting.

"David has the chicken pox. That's why I'm home today," the woman explained. "Obviously he couldn't go to school and his regular sitter couldn't take him, either. She has to think of the other children she cares for. Though they've probably been exposed by now anyway," she sighed. "I don't know why I'm

telling you all this. I guess I feel guilty about missing work."
She checked the flow of words to give Trout the opportunity to
state his purpose.

"I'd like to ask you some questions about Eve Galatea."

She shot a glance at David, who showed signs of opting for
the stranger's conversation. After tucking him up in the
blanket, she steered Trout into the dining area. She brought
two cups of coffee in from the kitchen and they sat at the table.

"I read about her death in the paper, poor thing," she spoke
in muted tones, her glance straying periodically to her patient
on the sofa. "The story tied it up to some inquest. She'd been a
witness or something."

"That's correct. Her death may or may not have been
connected. That's what I'd like to find out."

"I don't see how I can help, really. As far as I know she
hasn't—hadn't—been back to the building for more than a
month. She might have, I suppose, but I didn't see her. And she
did say she was taking a long vacation. We weren't close or
anything. She didn't write to me, if that's what you want to
know."

"No, I just want you to talk about her."

"I don't understand."

"I'm not sure I understand myself. I met her some days
before her death for reasons pertaining to the inquest you
mentioned. She puzzled me even then. I keep thinking if I can
unravel the mystery around her then finding her killer will be
easy—possible, anyway."

"I'm still not sure what you want me to tell you," Mrs.
Dorris said thoughtfully, running her palms back and forth on
her jeans.

"Well, Mrs. Lancaster described her as being sculpted entirely from dry ice."

"Oh, her!" she laughed. "She's such an old snoop. The day
after we moved in here she contrived some excuse for getting
in for a look around. Aspirin, I think it was. I showed her the
cabinet in the kitchen where I keep the medicines and then left
the room for something—I can't remember what. Anyway,

when I came back I found her poking around in a drawer. She said she was looking for a glass, you know—for water to wash down the aspirin. In a drawer! She's probably harmless, but I must say I'm glad I'm not home during the day. Eve didn't have a regular job that I know of and probably sensed the danger of continued visits from the start. You couldn't blame anyone for pulling in the welcome mat when Mrs. Lancaster's around."

"So you wouldn't describe Eve Galatea as unfriendly."

"Not unfriendly. Painfully shy, I think."

Shyness jibed far less with Trout's conception of Eve Galatea than hauteur. "Why do you say that?"

"I don't know, exactly. She was a very private person, but after a while she was quite cordial, too. Oh, I know," she brightened, "the first time I saw her was one morning as I was leaving for work. I was waiting for the elevator—why I can't tell you as the stairs are quicker and I could use the exercise— when the door opened. She was in a robe and was about to bend over for her newspaper when she noticed me. She was so embarrassed at not being dressed that she retreated without fetching her paper.

"I guessed, too, that she had been sick."

"Why?"

"Mostly from the way she overclothed herself. The way parents do with a first child," she looked fondly at the boy who had drifted off into a slightly fevered sleep. "You know: hat, extra sweater, scarves. That and her voice. It was hoarse and whispery the first few times I heard her speak. I know some of the other tenants attributed that to theatricality, but I suspect she had some kind of bronchial thing. And I'm sure I was right, because after a while she stopped dressing like an Eskimo and her voice was clear. She became more outgoing then, too. I think that was due to a combination of things: she was feeling better physically, and she'd become accustomed to living here, so she was able to overcome her shyness.

"I really can't tell you anything about her personal life. I never saw any of her friends."

"You've been a big help as it is," Trout said rising.

"I hope you find whoever did it. I didn't know Eve very well, but I liked her."

Upon reaching the corridor he turned back to express his wish for her son's swift recovery. With his back to the distant door of 301 and his hands clasped behind his back, he gave way to the acute desire to wave surreptitiously at the eyeball he felt boring in between his shoulder blades.

He met Mueller in the lobby and was informed that the manager's wife had come in.

His knock was answered instantly by a pinched-faced woman with the bearing of a crone in a stage play. Despite her tight mouth and drawn-in shoulders, Trout was struck by the realization that she was around the same age as Mrs. Dorris. The way she held her arms close at her sides and her chin tucked down nearly to her chest gave the impression that she was trying to offer the rest of the world the smallest possible target. Trout explained his purpose, and she looked harassed to the extreme.

"I know very little about any of the tenants. My husband takes care of all that. I'm an RN and I work a full shift at the hospital and do some private duty as well, not to mention keeping up our own rooms. Why don't you come back and talk to him? I'm expecting him around eight."

Trout leaned against the closing door. "I'll be back in Maine at eight."

"Then talk to Mueller. Nothing gets past him. You know, he's so proprietary about this place sometimes I wonder, when I'm coming home, if maybe this time he'll decide not to let me in. Of course I have my own key and he'd lose his job—I mean he *couldn't* do that kind of thing—but he's so quiet and . . . and judgmental. He makes me think of St. Peter at the gates. Imagine—he used to be a union organizer. It seems impossible—I mean he doesn't even speak. Oh, he'll answer you all right but nothing more." As though she too was unaccustomed to conversation, she seemed exhausted by this speech.

"I've already spoken with Mr. Mueller."

She looked wary now. "He made you think my husband could tell you things about Eve Galatea?"

"Not at all." Trout consoled himself with the thought that after each loony he had met that day his next encounter was with a sane, even likable person. He silently reminded the Fates that they owed him a winner to balance the score.

"I'm not home much. I can't be. We're trying to save enough money for a down payment on a house. I want to live in Belmont in my own home with a fenced-in yard. Is that so wrong? My husband isn't manager here; he's a slave. The tenants treat us like dirt and they call him anytime for anything. Someone can live with a dripping faucet for two weeks and then decide it must be taken care of during our dinner. If his mother weren't sick he'd be here now, putting up some old hag's curtain rod or fixing a disposal.

"Almost all the tenants here are women. Did you know that?" She waited for the full significance of her statement to sink in. "My husband says it's because of the building security, but I'm not a fool. He happens to be a very good-looking man," she said with a combination of pride of ownership and dismay. "And I'm off working and every day they're here finding excuses to get him up to their apartments, trying to get their hands on him. We've got to get out of this place." This last was said with the intonation of a litany. Trout half expected her to chant the line repetitively.

"I know nothing that would tie your husband to Eve Galatea, or any other resident, for that matter. At this point all I'm really interested in is viewing her apartment."

She was not convinced but relinquished her subject. "The Boston police already sent out somebody to look through her papers."

"I know that. I'm not concerned with her papers. I just want to look at the place where she lived."

"I guess that's all right," she said dubiously. "You won't take anything away, will you? I'll get the key." Then came a fresh outburst. "Though how we're supposed to rent the place with her stuff still in it I don't know."

Trout clucked sympathetically as she scrambled off to get the key. As she pressed it into his palm, she thrust her head forward in a chickenlike movement and whispered, "If you do find out something, about my husband, I mean, you'll let me know?"

Trout mumbled some assurance and the scrawny neck retracted. He fled to the stairs, declining the elevator out of fear that any delay might result in her accompanying him.

Strangely enough, he felt his arrival on the third floor to be unobserved. He let himself into Eve Galatea's apartment with a disproportionately profound sigh of relief. Though it was just afternoon, the front room was dark enough to warrant his flicking the light switch. The sudden illumination left him disappointed.

He wasn't sure what he had expected—a portrait of Eve over the mantle, a Ming vase in the corner, a writing table with a patina that bespoke the care of generations of Galateas. Instead he found a sparsely furnished room with achingly white walls. The walls held some adornment. The largest expanse fielded an enormous painting in a simple metal frame. It was all shapes, but not of the kind Trout thought of as abstract. There were dimensions and shadows. He checked the urge to touch its surface. The opposite wall bore a grouping of four lithographs, each inscribed with a title: Sloth, Gluttony, Lust, and Envy. Trout wondered what had happened to the other three deadly sins. He tried for some moments to recall the others but could only drag forth Pride from his memory. He assumed that these were masterfully done, but he heartily disliked them all the same.

The figures were twisted and deformed with bulging eyes and outsized mouths and hands, beak or snoutlike noses. It was a desecration of the senses. He was transfixed in repugnance by the depiction of Gluttony, which showed a tremendously obese trio of man, woman, and dog who, still unsated, amid the remains of a gargantuan feast were feeding on each other.

These and the large canvas on the opposite wall were the room's only ornaments. Near the door was a long slender table supporting a clock that had wound down and a lacquered bowl with a dry cleaning ticket in it. That stub was the only indication that life had existed in this rarefied atmosphere. The rest of the furnishings consisted of a full length grey sofa positioned in the middle of the room with a brass floor lamp at one arm and a small gateleg table at the other.

Enid would probably call it a tailored effect. Trout thought it looked unfinished and unfriendly, like the vestibule of a small but precious art gallery.

He proceeded to survey the remaining three rooms. The kitchen was well equipped if not spacious, and there had been just enough room to squeeze in a tiny table and a lone straight-backed chair. He opened a few cupboards, which held the customary kitchen necessities as well as some rather more exotic foodstuffs. A vial of carelessly replaced saffron tumbled off one of the shelves, prompting the memory of his unsuccessful attempt to grow saffron for Enid's unsurpassed bouillabaisse.

He remembered Enid dressed as she was when he had taken leave of her that morning—a short cotton robe, bare feet, tousled hair testifying to a fitful night. Almost simultaneously he pictured Eve moving through the apartment. In his mind's eye she was unchanging from dawn to dusk: well groomed— almost packaged—unyielding. Trout suddenly and most unexpectedly missed his wife.

He moved into a room to one side of the kitchen, which he assumed would serve most tenants as the dining area. It was a large light room with a bay of windows. It contained one overstuffed chair, an easel, tubes and brushes, and lots of canvases—some painted, some virgin. The floor was splattered with paint. The room had no draperies, just perfunctory shades. Two ashtrays overflowed—one on a window sill, the other onto the arm of the chair. Trout wondered if she shut herself off from the upheaval of this room or if she came in here to shut out the sterility of the rest of the apartment.

The unfinished work on the easel was a rendering of the facing windows with their faded shades. As Trout studied it he noticed that each casement apparently enclosed a different sky—morning, noon, and twilight, he supposed. He wondered if she had worked on each part at set times of the day. He wondered if the painting was any good.

He looked at the other canvases. There was a series of the chair. There were a few of details of the chair—a section of the wooden scrollwork rimming the back, a claw foot. There were some classic still lifes as well. He recognized the kitchen chair as the base for a display of the lacquered bowl and a linen towel. Clearly Eve had painted from life, and this one room seemed to provide the setting for as much life as she cared to portray.

Perhaps that explained her seclusion. And her emergence as well. Maybe she simply ran out of subject matter.

One canvas startled Trout. It was very different from the rest. A portrait. Of a man, he thought. Of even that he couldn't be sure. It was a disembodied head and very undefined. At first glance he took it as proof that at some time another person, a model, had been with her in this room. But unlike the other paintings, it was so vague and dreamlike in its effect that he decided she might well have created the person as well as the portrait.

He found the painting rather unsettling, but as the head was unable to speak, he declined to spend any more time with it. He crossed through the kitchen into the bedroom. The furnishings were luxurious enough but still managed to give the impression of asceticism.

There was an enormous bed in the center of the room with a commode and reading lamp to one side. The windows were heavily draped, and there was a small writing desk in a corner. Two walls were covered with books and the components of a costly stereo set. There wasn't a single paperback in evidence. There was a walk-through closet containing hanging clothes, accessories, and a narrow chest of drawers. It led into the bathroom, which also opened into the front room.

The bathroom contained nothing of interest to him. Its cabinets held a wide array of toilet articles and makeup brushes, a bottle of aspirin, an antiseptic ointment, some throat lozenges, and a thermometer. He was beginning to feel like a voyeur.

He stifled his rising suspicion of his own motives for being there and examined the contents of the chest of drawers. All clothing. He had one resource left. He drew open the single drawer of the desk and found her passport, birth certificate, the lease for the apartment, some notepaper and pens. He shut the drawer and sat heavily on the edge of the bed. There wasn't a photograph, a single memento among her belongings.

Trout heard footsteps in the front room.

He froze, waiting for the steps that had entered the kitchen to reach him, for the arrival that would explain everything. He was staring so intently at the doorway that a tear strained down his cheek.

It was the manager's wife. She had changed into a cocktail sort of dress, leaving too many buttons unbuttoned. She had layered herself with makeup, which made her look coarse as well as haggard, and her scent was so heavily applied that the fumes nearly toppled him off the bed.

The bed. He was momentarily bewildered, but as she stood there with a painted smile, he began to wish she had discovered him in any other room of the apartment, perched on any other piece of furniture.

Sauce for the goose, he supposed. He was to be the instrument of her revenge for all her husband's indiscretions, real or imagined.

He sprang catlike from the bed, dropping the key into her hand as he sidled past her into the kitchen. "Perfect timing. Just finished. You've saved me a trip. Thanks for your cooperation," he called as he cannoned out the front door.

He didn't pause to sigh his relief until he was back out on Merriweather happily breathing car exhaust.

Approximately an hour and a half later Trout reappeared at the door of 404 Merriweather, laden with bundles. He pressed the buzzer and, after a few moments, Mueller loomed into sight. His large features fell into a pattern of welcome as he ushered Trout in. Trout stealthily looked round and then wordlessly led the way to Mueller's alcove.

"Had to make sure there were no Furies about to pounce," Trout confided by way of explanation. "You most generously provided me with lunch. It is my pleasure to supply the dinner." He pulled a bottle of zubrovka from one paper sack and a parcel that proved to be a pot wrapped in toweling and layers of newspaper from another. He drew the protruding loaf of French bread from its wrapper and arranged the meal on Mueller's desk.

Mueller sniffed at the contents of the pot. "Bouillabaisse," said Trout. "And I had a hell of a time getting it, too. First I couldn't remember the name of the restaurant, but I knew it was around here somewhere. Then I had to convince them to sell me some. They frown on carryouts. Had to purchase the pot as well. I make a present of it to you," Trout said grandly.

Mueller came up with two mugs and a pair of carefully polished spoons for the soup, a third mug and a glass for the vodka. The food, the drink, the ambience were perfect. Trout gave the dinner three stars.

CHAPTER 8

Trout's exhilaration, or the liquor, warded off nervousness on his return flight. He even found himself warming to Hank Giroux.

He had purchased a second bottle of zubrovka, which he handed over to the burly pilot. "Instead of a thank you note," said Trout. Giroux grinned and Trout didn't even flinch when the pilot took a healthy swig from the bottle just prior to takeoff.

Giroux sang almost continuously while they were aloft. He had a clear lusty voice that filled the cabin of the plane. Most of the renditions were in French. Trout considered himself passably fluent in the language—he had studied it in school and could make himself understood overseas—but he always had trouble with the Canadian version. Different patterns or inflections or something.

They were performing an inharmonious duet of "Misty" when Giroux brought the plane in for landing.

Giroux ceremoniously decreed his intention to instruct Trout in the art of flying. With equal solemnity Trout insisted on delivering to Giroux some of his end-of-season excess—tomatoes, squash, gourds, pumpkins, some mum plants that needed thinning. They shook hands to commemorate the moment, and Trout drove off from the airfield wrapped in good feelings about the male sex, which had the ability to share things without turning them inside out.

Women worry at the fabric of a relationship, pulling, twisting, looking for flaws—that's what weakens it. He was very pleased with the profoundness of his perceptions.

By the time he arrived home he had a slight headache, which compounded his instinctive rage when he stumbled over a skateboard in the darkness. He lurched to his feet, looking for his attacker. When he located the culprit, he was torn between sheepishness at his reflexes and parental ire. He marched into the house, carrying the offending object before him like a stinking carcass.

Enid was sitting on the couch with her legs folded under her working a double acrostic. "Hullo. What's a by-product: five letters, second letter F?" She glanced up. "Oh! I'm sorry. Did you get hurt on that thing?"

"*You're* sorry?"

"Cannot tell a lie. I was using it on the driveway this afternoon. I guess I forgot to put it away." She dropped her head, awaiting the executioner's blow.

"How did you do?"

"Not very well, I'm afraid. But I plan to do better. I can see why the kids like it. It gave me the sensation of flying."

"Me, too."

"I *am* sorry."

"Hey, you know my return flight didn't bother me at all." There was an obvious note of pride in his voice. "Giroux has offered to give me flying lessons."

"Don't you think that's a bit risky?" she said dubiously.

"Probably a lot safer—for everybody—than your fooling

around on the skateboard. What inspired you, anyway?"

"I don't know. I guess I was feeling stolid and middle-aged. A small rebellion."

"Offal."

"What?"

"By-product in five letters."

"Oh . . . thanks. Yes, that fits. You always seem to know more than I expect you to."

"A compliment?"

"I think so."

"I'll take it. Where are the girls?"

"Upstairs."

"Aren't you going to tell me what you found in Boston?" Enid bleated indignantly.

"I'll be down in a minute. Patience isn't one of your strong points."

He started to mount the stairs when Enid voiced an involuntary "Oh!" He turned back. "Was that for me?"

"I'm afraid so. Agronski phoned this afternoon. I was to tell you to call him no matter what time you returned. I nearly forgot. Blame it on the skateboard."

"Damn. I wonder what Mr. Clean's uncovered now." He dialed the number with unreasonable irritation.

"Hello," came the agitated voice from the receiver.

"I understand you've got something for me."

"Thank God it's you, sir. I was beginning to think I couldn't sit on this information any longer."

"I'm listening."

"I think I can tell you who murdered Eve Galatea."

Trout's whole body tensed. "Go on, damn it."

"It was Nathan Adams."

Trout didn't say anything for a moment, and Agronski froze on the other end, leaving his last words hanging between them on the wire. "Son of a bitch," Trout finally sighed.

"Yessir." Agronski took that as his cue to continue. "I don't think there can be much doubt. You recall those two sets of prints, both identical, that I took off Miss Galatea's things at the cabin." He was hurrying now to cover his chagrin. "We had assumed, naturally enough, that those were Miss Galatea's prints. This morning I thought for form's sake I had better run them through the file. I knew she had no record, so I didn't expect a match, but then I got word from Augusta that the prints were Adams'."

"So how many people know that Adams is still alive?" Trout asked mechanically.

"No one else, sir. The assumption at the capitol was that I was doing some follow-up investigating on the suicide. I didn't contradict it. I wanted to hold off until you got back, but I don't mind saying I've been pretty nervous. I mean I'd hate to think he got away because of the delay."

"Yeah. Well, either he took off right after he got rid of her or he feels safe enough to hang around and watch us make fools of ourselves."

"You going to put out an all points?"

Trout hesitated, then said no very deliberately. "There was an A.P.B. on that bastard for over a year and we never even got close. I don't want him to know we know he's alive. Not yet, anyway. I'll just have to get out my violin and my pipe and meditate on the perfect entrapment."

"But what if he leaves the country? If we wait, we may lose him altogether."

"Don't be an idiot. If he wanted to leave the country he could have long ago. Remember, we're dealing with the original invisible man. Look," said Trout a little more patiently, "the man staged an elaborate suicide. Why? So we'd think he was dead. Why? So we'd stop looking for him. Why? So he wouldn't have to leave the country."

"Of course, sir, that must be right. Do you think there's any real chance of him being caught—locally, I mean?"

Trout knew that Agronski was making a valiant effort to stifle disapproval of his superior's unorthodox decision to conceal his discovery.

"I think there's a damn good chance that he's still around. His ego will hold him here until the thing's played out. His

ego's our only hope . . . You're sure you haven't mentioned this
to anyone?"

"Not even my wife."

"Good."

"Sir?"

"Yes?"

"Uh, about Homer . . ."

"Right. Informing him would be as good as taking a front
page ad."

"Yessir."

"What he doesn't know can't hurt us. Okay, use your brains
but try to bridle your initiative. Don't do anything without
checking with me first."

Trout held the receiver a long time before replacing it in its
cradle. He took the snifter of cognac that Enid held out to him:

"So Nathan Adams is alive and well and living in Fells
Harbor—Halesport County, anyway," she amended.

"Looks like it," he said dully.

"And he killed Eve Galatea?"

"Excellent deduction." Trout was watching her now, wondering what she was thinking.

"What's it all mean?" she asked a little too brightly.

"You know damn well what it means. It means she conspired
with him to fake his death. She knew him—though not well
enough, apparently."

"You don't know that. Maybe she thought she saw what she
said she saw." With effort Enid played devil's advocate. "She
never did claim to see the actual jump, did she? Maybe he killed
her for—I don't know—insurance. In detective stories innocent
witnesses are always being disposed of because of information
they aren't even aware they possess. There he was staging his
suicide and along comes this woman. She thinks he must have
killed himself but in fact she's seen something that proves he
hadn't, only she doesn't realize the significance of what she
saw."

Trout thought a moment, then picked up the receiver again.
His face was expressionless as he dialed the number.

"Gretchen? This is Trout. May I speak with Mrs. Adams please?" A minute passed tensely. "Mrs. Adams, I'm sorry to disturb you so late in the evening. Just a point of information I thought you might be able to help me with. Was your son a painter? . . . Still lifes mostly? . . . No, we're still trying to track down the money he embezzled. Thought we might be able to pin down where he'd spent the last year by circulating his photograph around art supply stores. Farfetched, I know, but we've got to try everything . . . Yes, thanks for your help."

Trout hung up and said, "Sooner or later, everything fits."

"What everything fits where?"

"Those first months that she lived in the apartment she was so aloof as to be unapproachable. It was mandatory that she keep people away. She didn't even speak. When the building's official busybody descended on her, she was not only inhospitable; she didn't even turn on the lights. Because there was something she didn't want seen. A pipe, perhaps, or a pair of men's slippers. Something. Maybe many things.

"And that other room. The apartment was so neat—sterile, even—but there was one room used as a studio and it was a disaster. And the subjects of all the paintings were there in that room. I was troubled by the canvas of the man. It was a self-portrait. He was living there with her all those months. Then when the hunt cooled and he made his headquarters elsewhere she seemed to warm up. Lost her shyness, overcame her struggle with laryngitis, or shed some of her hauteur, depending on your source."

"Why did he move out?"

"Maybe she was cutting too curious a figure with her hermit routine. It wouldn't have served their purpose to have attention of any sort focused on their apartment."

"What do you suppose was their relationship to each other?"

"Isn't that pretty obvious?"

"To you, maybe. I wouldn't ask if I knew." She sounded sincere. She didn't sound like she was enjoying rubbing salt into the wounds.

"They were lovers."

"But you said—it seems ages ago now—that Mrs. Adams had given you the definite impression that her son wasn't interested in women—sexually, I mean."

"Mothers aren't always the best judge of such matters. It was a one-bedroom apartment. With the funds he had available they didn't choose it with economy in mind."

"I suppose not."

"What I can't figure out is why she didn't say she'd actually seen him jump. Why all that business about driving on and the car mirror?"

"I can understand that on a couple of counts. Maybe they didn't want it to sound too pat. After all, she didn't need to claim to see the jump to make it believable. They chose their location carefully. Unless she was lying, he had to have jumped—there just wasn't any place else he could be. And look at the simplicity of it. People get caught up in their lies when they add too much detail. This way she wouldn't be expected to know the exact spot where he went over, whether he flailed his arms. She couldn't embellish so she couldn't make mistakes."

"Makes sense. Yeah, it really does. It was one of the things that lent credibility to her description—worrying about handling that curve before the turnoff to the old cannery, the idle glance in the mirror, the confusion at his disappearance, and the startling realization." Trout laughed, but it had a nasty edge to it. "You know, I remember asking her that first day if she was an actress."

"She duped the coroner and the coroner's jury, the federal investigators, the press. You weren't the only one."

"Yeah, but there are degrees in these things."

There followed an unpleasant lull in which the past weeks and their accompanying emotions seemed to wash over them both. There was a short distance between them, which Enid tried to bridge.

"I wonder what made him shoot her?"

Her effort didn't span the gap.

"I don't give a damn," said Trout.

Trout was shuffling the papers on his desk. It was littered
with random notes—on the information Eve Galatea had given
him the day of the "suicide," on Gretchen Bergstrom, on the
timetable of those present at the Hornsby house the night of the
shooting, on the interviews from the previous day in Boston.
With one grand gesture he swept the whole mass off the top
and into a drawer.

He still felt Gretchen was the key to the puzzle. Even if she
hadn't killed Eve Galatea, she knew something that she was
hiding. Maybe her behavior at the inquest resulted from certain
knowledge that Nathan Adams was very much alive. Perhaps
she had seen him or been contacted by him, aided him in some
way. Obviously she hadn't been in on the faking of his death or
Eve Galatea's testimony would not have startled her. But if she
knew that Nathan Adams was alive, she was probably the only
person who might know where he could be found.

Trout's feelings of frustration were at an all-time high. He
couldn't push Gretchen. He couldn't let on that he knew
anything at all. No wonder she had called him a fool. He had
been looking for Eve Galatea's murderer, and her murderer
was a dead man.

God, how he hated Eve Galatea for that. It wasn't that she
had lied to him but that she had made him love it. The whole
thing was one bloody personal insult. She had deserved her
death—the betrayal of it, anyway. He grew angry whenever he
thought of her.

He felt differently about Nathan Adams. He told himself he
wanted to catch him because no man was above the law: you
can't let a murderer and embezzler roam free. He couldn't
admit that he was driven to discover the fascination this man
held for Eve Galatea.

He was short-tempered with Enid that morning for her
complete about-face. She had been contemptuous of Eve Galatea when she thought her above suspicion. Now that she knew
of her complicity she was romanticizing her. She had cate-
chized that Eve Galatea had lied to protect someone she loved.
And that Nathan Adams had ruthlessly killed someone who

loved him. As if anything were ever that simple.

Trout indulged himself in a spate of self-pity. He was feeling lonely, misunderstood, and unappreciated and was trying to determine whether these sentiments were endemic to his job, the state of matrimony, or the awareness of encroaching age when a considerably more aged head appeared above his desk.

"Good morning," George Cox said perfunctorily.

"Not at all," mumbled Trout in reply. "Sorry," he said, grasping the other man's hand and guiding him to the vacant chair. "How have you been, George?"

"Well, thank you."

"Not a social call, I gather."

"No."

"I tried to reach you in Bangor. Spent yesterday in Boston myself."

"I know."

"Well, um, what's up?"

"How far are you from solving this Galatea killing?"

"Between you and me and the bedpost, it's solved. Murderer's still at large, though."

"Thank God." Great relief—and, characteristically, not a glimmer of curiosity—passed over George Cox and seemed to warm his body so that the icy tension melted from his voice.

"What are you celebrating?" Trout couldn't recall ever seeing such a panoramic grin stretched across the medical examiner's face.

"Not the escape, I can assure you."

"Don't be so coy, George. It's not becoming."

George's booming voice dropped so that Trout had to strain forward to pick up his words. "In the course of my examinations I uncovered some . . . information. I admit I was baffled. That's what prompted my trip to Bangor—I wanted to consult with a doctor I know there."

"You couldn't have done it by phone?" Trout probed.

"No, I couldn't."

"And?"

"I'm old-fashioned. I expect you know that by now. That

means I'm not only thorough but I have certain scruples."

"What are we talking about, George?"

"As I said, some information came to light. Of a highly controversial nature. At first I didn't understand it—that comes from being old-fashioned, too, I suppose," he sighed. "Once it was confirmed for me I had to decide what to do with this information."

"*What* information?"

"I can't tell you that."

"You *what?*"

"That was the decision I reached. Look, I promise that knowing it could not possibly lead you to the location of the murderer. It was feasible, though only slightly, that it might aid you in determining the identity of the killer. In the event that identity was still unknown to you I was prepared to consider giving you the information. But, even then, I had in no way made up my mind to do so. Your diligence in attaching a name to the criminal has removed a great responsibility from my shoulders."

"You're crazy, George. You really are."

"I'm sorry you feel that way." He stiffened in his chair.

"I'm sorry," said Trout in an effort to soothe Cox's ruffled dignity, "but you know you can't withhold anything in a current murder case. You're the medical examiner and I'm the sheriff, for godsakes."

"Perhaps we perceive the responsibilities of my job differently," Cox responded coolly.

"Yes, I'd say you're to assist in an investigation, not hamper it."

"And I'll say again that this information is not pertinent to the investigation. There is nothing to add about the circumstances of her death. I consider it my duty as a physician and a moral member of the community to avert scandal and gossip."

"But it's your duty as medical examiner to give me *all* the facts."

"All the pertinent facts."

"I suppose I'll just have to call someone else in on this case. I'm sure the coroner would concur."

"If that's your feeling, I'll have my resignation ready by the morning."

Trout sighed again, most profoundly. "Let's not either of us be too hasty, George. We'll both think it over. Maybe on further reflection you'll be able to tell me . . . whatever it is. Or there might be some kind of compromise . . ."

"A compromise is hardly possible." Cox turned back at the door. "Sophie asked me to tell you that she'd delighted to accept Enid's offer to bring along a pot of her baked beans."

"Beans?"

"The Labor Day picnic."

"Sure. Of course. My love to Sophie."

"Yes." With that briefest of farewells, the white-domed monument to Truth, Justice, and the American Way was gone.

Homer stuck his head in the door, ostensibly for any instructions Trout might have to give him, but really to learn what the ruckus was all about.

"Who was that masked man?" Trout shouted gaily. Homer blinked twice and sidled back toward his own desk.

"Crusty old fart," Trout said softly.

"I really am grateful to you for coming."

Enid acknowledged receipt of these words with a nod of the head. Her mouth was busy with a triple-decker turkey sandwich.

"I know I've made you unhappy lately."

Enid shrugged and sawed off a piece of protruding tomato with her teeth.

"I've been unhappy, too, and I think the chief reason is that we stopped talking."

Enid chewed thoughtfully.

"If we hadn't been out of communication we would have avoided the whole thing. I mean, we started living separate lives—in our imaginations, anyway. We acted like strangers."

Enid worried at a piece of lettuce.

"I'm glad it's behind us now. I really need to talk with you."

Enid sucked deliberately on her pickle.

"Cox came to me with an announcement that he has discov-

ered something bizarre in the course of the autopsy. He insists
that it has no bearing on the murder and he righteously refuses
to inform me of his findings. Doesn't want to go down in the
annals of science as a thrill mongerer. So what do I do? You
know how impossible he is. The more I badger him, the more
stiff-necked and tight-assed he'll become. If I call in someone
else, he says he'll resign. The information probably isn't central
to the case—he's convinced it isn't and he's not stupid. What
really infuriates me is that the bastard doesn't trust my discretion."

At the word "discretion" Enid's eyebrows arched over her
coffee mug.

"Be fair," Trout pleaded.

Enid strove to look fair while nibbling methodically on a
French fry.

She cleared her mouth, dabbed its corners, and wiped each
finger with the paper napkin. "You want his resignation and
you want to feel you have my support?"

"I don't know. No, I don't want him to resign. Forcing him
to do that seems tantamount to murder somehow."

"You want me to say that you wouldn't be forcing him? That
it's his choice? That he's forcing you?"

"No," he barked, suspecting that was precisely what he
wanted her to say. "Will you quit acting like a goddam
therapist? Let's leave my psyche intact and analyze the situation
instead."

"Maybe George will change his mind."

"Do you think so?"

"Not in the least. George never changes his mind. 'Why
tamper with perfection?' I think that's inscribed on his family
crest."

"What would you do?"

"Talk to Sophie, I guess."

"I thought of that. She's too . . . virginal."

"Naive, you mean?"

"No. Naive virgins aren't virgins very long. These days I
equate virginity with fierce determination—blind faith in the
great value of something that everyone else prices with small

change. If Cox is going to stand on his principles, Sophie is going to stand behind him."

"What do you think this mysterious information could be?"

"Needle tracks. Pregnancy. Rape prior to the shooting, or," he shuddered, "afterwards. I don't know. It's impossible to tell with a man like George. It could be something horrific, or, with his Victorian sensibilities, it could be that she went about without a bra.

"It's not as though she has any family to distress with unsavory revelations," he resumed in injured tones. "And it's insulting on his part to assume that I would make the information public in the first place."

"But dirt does have a way of turning up in the most unlikely quarters."

"What do you mean?"

"George tells you. You tell me and Agronski. He tells his wife . . ."

"Agronski never tells his wife anything but what he wants for dinner."

"Too bad. Then you'd know I leaked it unless you were suspicious of yourself."

"Get serious."

"I am, in a way. Why do you need to know? You already know who killed her. I think it's rather fine of George to shoulder whatever ugliness he thinks would unnecessarily burden the rest of us."

"But I'm the sheriff," Trout roared, bringing the waitress scurrying back to replenish their coffee. "It's my job to know everything about a case I'm working on," he continued in muted tones after her departure.

"Wait a couple days before coming to a decision. Maybe you'll catch Nathan Adams and you won't have to decide at all."

"But it's the principle of the thing," Trout pouted.

"I count myself among the privileged—knowing two such principled men," Enid commented blandly.

Trout eyed her suspiciously, then decided whatever her intent, she was rather lucky at that.

CHAPTER 9

It was a glorious day for the Labor Day picnic, wonderfully cool and clear—perfect for the fires that would dot the beach by George and Sophie's house. The house itself was ideal for the annual tradition. It was weathered and ramshackle but sturdy against the winds and wet that had battered its gables and chimneys over the years. The house had not had its complement of children in George and Sophie's time. Trout thought the picnic was their way of filling it with voices and activity that would echo through the rooms until the next year's gathering. Since Sophie was denied motherhood, she took the entire town to her breast and George, though he might have made a difficult father, was superb in the role of patriarch.

The picnic was the undisputed social event of the year, not that there was any vying for invitations. The whole town was invited and the whole town came, as well as folk from surrounding communities. Except for a handful of stragglers, all the summer people had packed their fishing rods, tanning oils, motorbikes, and bug sprays and clanked back to their respective cities. Summer was officially over, and the year-round residents assembled to celebrate their release.

Many operated seasonal businesses; most retail stores—craft shops, book stores, bike and boat rentals, even the bulk of clothing and grocery stores and restaurants—would be closed now until May. Owners wouldn't make enough in the off season to defray heating expenses.

The natives were accepting of their dependence on the tourist trade. There was no hostility toward the seasonal waves of folk with dollars to spend. There was, however, a nearly audible sigh of collective relief at their departure. The occasion of the picnic served to separate "them" from "us." The renewed solidarity wasn't spoken of, it was a simple fact that one recognizes, like the change of seasons that heralded it.

No one arrived empty-handed. Enid's contribution of baked beans filled a lobster pot. Fishermen brought their catch. There were home-baked breads and pies, corn for roasting, cakes and preserves, and a variety of miscellaneous specialties from local kitchens. To date no one could claim to have ever managed to sample everything at these gatherings. George and Sophie provided the beverages. There was always enough beer and lemonade to displace the water in the harbor and George was adept at mixing a rum punch that was served from a spotless old porcelain bathtub kept solely for that purpose. Though they might be the preeminent conservatives of Fells Harbor—or all of Halesport County, for that matter—the Coxes were very liberal with their liquor on Labor Day. For the sober-minded they borrowed large urns from the restaurants, which were kept filled with piping hot coffee and teas. It was a feast that began sometime before noon and usually ended with a surprisingly large group of diehards greeting the sunrise on the cold September beach.

Enid and the girls had come over in the morning with a supply of firewood in the station wagon to help Sophie set up and to run any last minute errands.

Trout remained in his office until six o'clock when Homer

grudgingly relieved him. He smelled of beer and when he belched obligingly in Trout's face, the sheriff got a preview of the banquet awaiting him.

"I don't see why anybody's got to be here," Homer said with heartfelt self-pity. "Everybody is at the picnic and everything in town is closed up. If we're needed anywhere it's at the beach—you know, to prevent a fight or something if somebody has too much to drink." He belched again for emphasis.

"Homer, I'm surprised at you. This is when we must be our most vigilant. As you say, it's like a ghost town around here— the perfect setting for looting or vandalism. It's your responsibility to see that no burglary or arson occurs. How would it look if the law enforcement representatives of the county were all partying it up while a lone maniac wandered the streets unhampered, burning the town to the ground?"

Homer was a susceptible young man in his normal state, and he had consumed enough alcohol to lend fire to his imagination. Trout could almost see Homer's vision: Homer and a vicious psychopath alternately stalking each other on the deserted streets of Fells Harbor.

"And don't forget Eve Galatea's killer is still at large." Trout felt himself completely avenged for all Homer's past transgressions as he watched the other's eyes involuntarily search the corners and examine the shadows.

As Trout drove toward the beach he calmed his conscience by reminding it that someone really did need to be on call, and he had doubtless saved Homer from a roaring drunk and a racking hangover.

The coast road in the vicinity of the Coxes' house was lined with parked cars. For quite a length only one lane was open for driving. Trout parked at the extreme closest to town. As a youth he had intuited the intrinsic value of the fast getaway. He was one of those who sit on the aisle at the movie theater and plant themselves by the door on the bus. However, on this occasion he was also trying to delay a confrontation with George Cox, at least until he resolved the course it should take in his own mind. His steps fell slower as he approached the house.

His hesitancy proved unnecessary as the object of his consternation was nowhere to be seen in its environs. Trout was reprieved until his host saw fit to roll in from the beach.

He surveyed the downstairs swollen with people. He was struck by the idea of a sausage casing expanding as it was stuffed. After observing for a few moments, he realized that the impression of elasticity was maintained by the spilling out of guests onto the beach through the side door as latecomers, or those desirous of a change of scene, squeezed in at the back. It was as if movement were carefully regulated by unseen pulleys and internal clocks.

He was trying to make his way toward Sophie, who was engaged in animated conversation with a vaguely familiar back on the other side of the room. His efforts were less than useless. They earned him reproachful glances from those whose movements instinctively followed the pattern established by the crowd. He found himself shouldered into a corner, which mercifully contained a keg of beer and suitable plastic containers.

Trout fortified himself and with refill in hand turned to participate in the conversation that had located at his elbow. Norman Collier clasped a welcoming if somewhat unsteady arm around Trout's shoulder while shooting a look of defiance toward his wife. She was the embodiment of rebuke, dressed in a neat cotton jumper (which Trout decided with a regrettable giggle didn't have the nerve to wrinkle on her body) holding amidst the sea of disposable plastic and paper a china cup and saucer which, Trout noted, despite the jostling throng, remained dripless.

"Have you seen Enid?" he asked. "Just arrived myself. Been working." He nearly apologized under Alice's stern eye.

"She's on the beach. One of the few that braved the water. Quite a girl," Norm said wistfully. "You know, when we were kids—"

"Save it for Enid," Alice snapped. "Why don't you get yourself another drink and go find her? Then the two of you can reminisce until the sun comes up." She pivoted and, just before the parting crowd swallowed her up, Trout impulsively and decidedly goosed her. She gave a small cry and turned back as she fixed her angry and suspicious gaze on Trout. He met her look with a profoundly blank one of his own. To his surprise her glance softened as it rested on him. He noticed with grudging admiration that she still hadn't spilled any of her coffee, then she moved away quickly. She had no trouble threading her way across the room.

Norman had been unaware of the preceding transaction. He suspected that he had been insulted, but his overriding state was one of confusion. He excused himself and went off in search of Alice, or Enid.

Trout's gaze returned to Sophie Cox. He could see now that the woman with whom she was speaking was Gretchen Bergstrom. As though picking his way through a maze, he maneuvered across the room, taking note of the presence of Mrs. Hornsby Adams and Dr. Cutter along his path. By the time he had arrived at his destination, Sophie had already turned away and connected with a small group arguing the merits of offshore drilling. Trout and Gretchen found themselves face to face and thoroughly alone as happens in crowded noisy rooms. The space around them was small but inviolable. They spoke quietly. Trout was a little surprised that they didn't have to shout.

"Hello," Gretchen said, "I was wondering where you were."

"Keeping America safe."

"And what's to become of it now?"

"I'm easily replaced. Homer Caulfield is presently protecting our wealth and welfare."

Her face clouded over. "He was here earlier, wasn't he? He kept watching me. Sneering, rather. It was such a silly freckled face with such a hard cruel look on it."

"He drank too much beer."

"Oh. I suppose so."

Gretchen glanced nervously around the room, and Trout thought she was a pleasant-looking woman and that it was perverse of him not to have noticed it before. She had a longish dress on, of a color between mauve and champagne. It was a shirtwaist kind of thing, tailored and proper but with yards and yards of fabric billowing out from her waist, reminding Trout of a sea nymph rising from the pale mists.

She looked now as if she'd like nothing better than to sink back into them. He could see that she was searching for an escape from him.

Not waiting for a protest, Trout took her empty glass and authoritatively parted the crowd, returning with two drinks before she could manage to disappear.

"I'm surprised to find you here—I mean at the party," he said as she rapidly half-emptied her glass.

"Being the hired help, you mean?" she said coolly. "It's a very egalitarian gathering."

"No, not at all. It's just that I've been coming to these Labor Day extravaganzas for years and have never found anyone from the Hornsby house in attendance before."

"Oh. Like the rest of the summer people, we always fold up our tent and retreat before Labor Day. This year has been— exceptional, as you know."

"I'm glad you could come."

"It's a lovely party."

The sudden silence between them seemed to overpower the surrounding din.

"I expect we'll be leaving in a few days." Her voice was tentative, questioning.

"I hope to have the case under wraps by then," Trout said smoothly with watchful eyes under his lowered lids.

Gretchen had started violently.

"I have some new information about Nathan Adams," he added conspiratorially.

"What do you mean?"

"Look, I understand the divided loyalties that have made you keep silent, but look at what those same divided loyalties have cost you. You came perilously close to losing your life or your sanity."

Her absolute stillness was her assent. Trout felt encouraged.

"You can't think much of Nathan Adams now."

"I detest the very thought of him." She said this so readily and so calmly that Trout was momentarily taken aback.

"I know the suicide was a sham," he continued. "And," he paused, then plunged, "I know who the murderer is."

"Then you must realize the case can never be closed." She was pleading with him. "Nathan was never worth the suffering he caused everyone. You must see that. It has to stop."

Trout couldn't see a thing. He felt transported through the looking glass into the middle of someone else's chess game and Gretchen had become the Red Queen. One step forward, two squares back.

"Eve Galatea's murderer can't go free, not to spare anyone. You must see that."

"*Her* murderer?" Gretchen looked at him with unbridled loathing. "I think perhaps of all of us you are quite the maddest."

She knew a good exit line when she barked one, Trout thought as he watched her spin off, her skirts struggling to catch up with her.

In his bewilderment he had failed to notice the appearance of Sophie Cox at his left elbow. At his elbow was doubly appropriate in this case as it served to indicate her height as well as her location. Trout was often a little startled when he saw her standing at close range—the schoolboy in him refused to allow her towering image to dwindle to her diminutive proportions. She touched his arm gently and he reeled upon her, ready to face an opponent.

"What was that all about?" they queried in unison.

"I thought I was lining up a witness for the prosecution. Instead I found myself in the dock."

"Sounds very confusing."

"'Twas. We couldn't seem to settle on our roles. Both of us wanted to play Alice to the other's March Hare."

"You're not the least bit off-putting, you know. It was about the Galatea murder and I think it's beastly of you to use my home for your interrogations."

"I'm sorry. Sort of," he amended. "It's all your doing anyway. This was the last place I expected to encounter the Hornsby-Adams cast of characters. I thought for a moment you arranged this by way of reparation for George's adamant silence about his mysterious findings."

"Not at all."

"Then you are aware of our—professional dispute?"

"Of course. Not the nature of it, though, so it's no use pumping me."

"Even if you could tell me, I know you wouldn't," he sighed. "You're as mulishly loyal as he is stubborn."

"How you do turn a phrase."

"Forgive me, Sophie. I'm out of sorts. The rest of the world can despise me, they can queue up for miles just for the opportunity to snub me, but I need you on my side. Your good opinion is necessary to my survival."

"Such a burden. You have it, then."

He bowed in humble acceptance of the royal boon. "But what are these people doing here?"

"Enjoying themselves, I trust. And they'll continue to do so if you stop pestering them."

"Now, really," he wheedled, "why were they invited?"

"Mildred and I go back a good many years. We did war work together. Everything from bonds to rolling bandages. We see each other from time to time. Since they were staying on in Fells Harbor for yet a while it seemed only natural to ask her and Gerald and Miss Bergstrom to join us today."

"And Dr. Cutter?"

"That was George's doing. He met him at the inquest, I believe. Ran across him since and invited him. Disappointingly simple and aboveboard. Nothing sinister here except your determination to make a nuisance of yourself." She whirled to include a passing guest in their conversation. "Am I not correct, Gerald?"

"I'm sure you are, Mrs. Cox. You are unfailingly correct."

"Thank you, Gerald. Gerald can always be depended on to find the right response to any situation." She inclined her head back toward Trout. "Unlike you, dear, Gerald and I prize discretion." She patted their arms as though encouraging them to settle a playground dispute and took herself off in the direction of the kitchen.

"A wonderful woman," Gerald said rather woodenly.

"The best," Trout agreed.

"Perhaps we ought to confine our conversation to her."

"Delighted."

"See here, Trout. You thoroughly upset Gretchen. That was apparent from the other side of the room. Was there really any need for that? Can't you—behave?"

Taken by itself, his last word sounded rather lame, but Gerald managed to weigh it down portentously with implications of breeding, culture, and etiquette.

"Gerald, I don't know how to get answers without asking questions."

"You must leave her alone. She's so fragile."

"Gretchen?" Trout came dangerously close to snorting, but, under the influence of Gerald's earnest sincerity, he coaxed his features into the bland smile of a game show host. "Of course you mean the wrist-slashing business. I guess my interpretation differs somewhat from your own. I think that she is indeed more affected than most by—things. But not passively, fragilely so. She takes strong action."

"If she were as strong as you claim, she'd be dead now."

"The suicide attempt of a strong person ends in a successful suicide? You do have a point. What most interests me, on a purely personal level, is the intensity of your desire to protect her." Gerald looked away, scowling. "I mean no insult to the lady, but she is an unlikely Helen of Troy. Yet think of the suitors she inspires. There was some kind of romance with your brother Nathan. Cutter has been pining after her for donkeys' years. And now you seem to have taken up the standard. It's a goddam epidemic."

Suddenly Trout was reminded of that first day—the day he had met Eve Galatea—when he told Gerald of his brother's death and Gerald had searched for an avenue of escape. The same rabbity desire to withdraw was there again for anyone to read in his darting eyes.

"Did you know then, that day"—Trout didn't need to explain what day as they both apparently had the same one in mind—"that your brother was still very much alive?"

"Do you like anagrams? Live, vile, evil."

"Did you know about the pretended suicide? You didn't really believe that Nathan was dead."

"When you've waited a lifetime for something, it's very difficult to believe the waiting is over. It's the waiting itself that becomes real, not the thing awaited.

"For purposes of illumination," Gerald had clearly recovered himself, "let's say there are two kinds of people in the world. Both kinds are impoverished. You have to grant that or I can't go on. Both are impoverished, and both are given the object of their heart's desire, and both experience a fleeting moment of rapture. Then type A accepts it and incorporates it into his life-style so readily that it seems to make no difference. The awe and appreciation are gone, being replaced by heretofore un-thought of needs. So type A is still and ever impoverished, still grasping. Type B can't believe his great good luck. Really can't believe it. So he encases his treasure in a vault where the vagaries of weather or Wall Street or his own whim, can't penetrate, and he might as well have never received it. I'm type B. I couldn't believe you unless I touched the corpse. And even then I'd have my doubts."

"You never fail to astound. I have no glimmer of what you will be when you pull yourself out of the hat from one time to the next. So because of your bankrupt spirit you were not altogether convinced of your good fortune when I told you of Nathan's suicide. And yet again, while considerably less enthu-siastic, you were perhaps even more disbelieving when you discovered that he was still alive. Have I got it?"

"When did I make this discovery?" Gerald said, eyebrows raised.

"I wish I knew. I wish to hell I knew."

"That's important, is it?"

"It is to me."

"Just what do you think you have?"

"The identity of the murderer of Eve Galatea."

For a moment Trout thought Gerald was going to scream involuntarily, but his face paled and his mouth went slack. "How long have you known?" he said finally, heavily.

"Not long."

"Why are you waiting? Finish it." His voice was rising. Trout thought he would scream now. Not in surprise but in anger. Heads were beginning to turn in their direction. With effort Gerald resumed the tight control of a corporation head at a board meeting. When they were no longer objects of interest to their fellow revelers, he said, almost smiling, "It's a matter of proof, then?"

"No. I think we're pretty well provided for in that area."

"Then why are you standing here? Talking to me?"

"I'm not on duty tonight." Trout was trying to be flippant and doing, he knew, a poor job of it. But he wanted to keep Gerald talking. The man was in possession of some very volatile information. He obviously believed Trout was also in possession of it. If he could just be kept talking it would explode from him. Trout wondered with a rising shiver of excitement if it was the location of Nathan Adams that Gerald supposed to be their shared truth. He was trying to determine the best method of probing this possibility, of stringing Gerald along until he blundered into a concrete admission of their common knowledge, when his thoughts were interrupted by an alarming and disarmingly grateful cast to Gerald's eyes and catch in his voice.

"This was a warning, then." Trout wondered if Gerald believed his brother was gunning for him. "I appreciate it but, unlike my brother, I won't hide."

He found his hand being warmly clasped by Gerald, who then edged off into the press of bodies.

Trout blinked rapidly as though mechanically feeding his brain each flimsy piece of information, each assessment. Then standing there in the middle of that overcrowded room, he closed his eyes and waited for the answer, but it didn't compute. It was impossible to add up because he couldn't determine the common, or uncommon, denominator. He felt he had all the pertinent data but lacked the key, the code that would make sense of it all.

He opened his eyes to reveal the owner of the hand laid lightly upon his arm. Mildred Hornsby Adams stood before him with her other hand cradled over the elaborately carved head of a walking stick.

"You seem to be provoking the various members of my household to flight." Her tone was, despite her age and the rigidity of her bearing, nothing if not flirtatious. But her eyes belied her voice. She was examining Trout carefully. After a thorough scrutiny during which Trout had to restrain the sudden impulse to check his fly, she said with the quiet authority of a magistrate, "You know something that you should tell me."

"Truth be told, Mrs. Adams, I don't know what I know. That's the profound conclusion I just reached. There are a lot of people who seem to know more about this case than I do. Are you one of them?"

"I know that Gretchen is incapable of murder."

"Life would be unbearable if each of us couldn't claim a few people who would make that testimonial about us, but unfortunately no one is incapable of murder. No one I've met, anyway." He felt an immediate sharp pang of remorse as he saw the anxiety spread across her face. Kick an old woman while she's down, he thought. "I don't think Gretchen did it, Mrs. Adams. Not any more."

She studied him again, then nodded. "Thank you. I see Dr. Cutter is approaching. How weary you must be growing of us all. I hope you'll find some chance to enjoy yourself tonight. Good evening, Doctor. Mr. Trout."

Before Trout could ferret out an appropriate hackneyed phrase Mrs. Adams had turned and, with a mobility that made one doubt her age and dependence on her cane, sailed through the throng that parted in advance of her.

Her place at Trout's side was instantly appropriated by
Cutter. Trout felt as though he were standing beside an invisible conveyor belt whose function it was to transport each
member of the Hornsby Adams entourage into his presence in
quick succession. He allowed himself to wonder whether Nathan Adams too might finally be deposited at his elbow if he
maintained his position. The image of the man, running hard
just to stay in place and being defeated by the inexorable steady
movement of the treadmill, was dissolved by Cutter's uncharacteristically hearty greeting.

"Trout, I'm glad you're here. No, really. I want to apologize. I was a real bastard the other day in my office. No, I
was." Trout hadn't disagreed. "I was upset. You can understand that. Say, I met your wife. She's lovely. Really lovely.
Not just to look at. She's got a kind of earthy quality, you
know? Looks like a born breeder. My professional opinion. No
charge." Trout was beginning to hope the floor would open up
and swallow one of them. "Anyway, you can just imagine how
you'd react if someone came to you with a variety of ugly
assumptions about her." Trout was afraid that the garrulous
effects of the alcohol were fading and Cutter was going to go
maudlin on him now. "I mean, you know her and you love her,
and you wouldn't want some stranger impugning her honor.
You do understand, don't you?"

Rather to his surprise, Trout did understand perfectly well.

Trout clasped Cutter on the shoulder in a spontaneous burst
of sympathy, which brought Cutter's gaze down. "We're
empty," he announced solemnly. So, with Trout's arm still
engaged around the doctor's shoulders, the two weaved and
bobbed to the impromptu bar in the corner, filled their cups,
and weaved and bobbed again until they discovered themselves
out front propped against a car parked askew in the driveway.

Cutter removed his hand from inside his jacket and produced
an unopened bottle of rum. "Didn't see me liberate this, did
you?" he asked with some pride. "Doctor's got to be quick
with his hands," he confided. "Anyway, I rescued it from
dilution with fruit juice."

They drained their beers and started on the warm straight rum.

"I want to straighten you out. I don't know anything 'cept what I told you. I don't know who killed the Galatea woman. I do know it wasn't Gretchen. I did check on her that night and she was asleep. Honest. She looked so small and helpless lying in that bed. I must have imagined her lying in bed a thousand times. Probably every night for years now." He cut himself off. "If you don't believe me, you can just go to hell," he said in a voice gruff with alcohol and emotion.

"I believe you," Trout said.

"Hey, that's great. That's really great." Cutter beamed at him affectionately and measured out two more doses of rum.

"Sometimes," he said, staring into the viscous pool in his plastic glass, "sometimes I wish I'd never met her. Better to marry than to burn, right? I'd say so. I've been burning for seven years now. Should make the *Guinness Book*. I'm boring you. Sorry."

"Not at all." Trout felt genuine compassion for Cutter— wanted him to enjoy the catharsis of an inebriated unburdening—but still couldn't comprehend his enduring fascination with Gretchen. "How did you meet her?" Trout thought the question an inept attempt to bridge the silence that had fallen between them, but Cutter turned an eager face to his.

"I've often wondered how much I was affected by our first meeting. It was about a year after I'd come here. Escaping, I guess, from a brief marriage and what was for me a pretty bewildering divorce. Anyway, I kept much to myself. Immersion in work and all that. And there was plenty of work to keep me busy. Not that I'm saying I was a highly sought social trophy, but I managed to beg off from most of the invitations I did receive.

"That's why it's so odd that we met in the first place. It was a costume ball. Can't imagine why I accepted. Wasn't my sort of thing at all. Maybe I welcomed an opportunity to wear a mask. Funny—I can't recall what I went dressed as.

"I can remember that the arrivals seemed to have ceased some time before and I was feeling restless and self-conscious and contemplating my departure. And then on the landing above the ballroom there appeared this magnificent tableau: Launcelot, Guinevere, the Lady of the Lake, and the Lady of Shallot.

"Probably sounds ridiculous to you, but I was terribly struck by that picture of Launcelot and his three ladies. Anyway, I changed my mind about leaving.

"Gerald was Launcelot, of course. His build alone was enough to assure anyone he was the strongest knight in Camelot. Mrs. Adams was convincing as the foster mother Lady of the Lake. I don't know if it's money or breeding, but there's something otherworldly about her even when she's having her blood pressure checked. And you can imagine my surprise when fifteen minutes into a conversation with Guinevere she revealed that she was Nathan, but then I had never run into him before so I had no reason to guess. But the one who captured my eye and my heart, spake the uninspired poet, was the fair Lady of Shallot.

"Gretchen was perfection." Cutter had imbibed enough so that these two words rhymed as he solemnly and thickly pronounced them, but he didn't seem to notice. "She was so sweet and melancholy. It was impossible not to believe she was pining away for some secret love."

"And you've been playing the Lady of Shallot to her Launcelot ever since," Trout spoke in annoyance before he could stop himself.

"Listen, you bloody—oh, damn. Yes, well, I suppose I have." Cutter's anger melted as quickly as it had erupted. "I wasn't such an ass from the start, though. I mean, Gretchen seemed to enjoy being with me. And even on that first evening Mrs. Adams seemed to be pleased with my attentions in that direction.

"I don't know. Maybe the thing would have run its course, but Mildred Hornsby Adams," he bowed his head in obeisance, "has spent years comforting me that all Gretchen needed was a little more time. You know, I think she took me on as her personal physician to give me opportunities to see Gretchen or maybe to have Gretchen see me. After a time I became a regular recipient of dinner invitations. I shouldn't complain. I was well fed and well paid."

"Was?"

"She told me tonight that they'll probably be selling the Hornsby house. Money is definitely an object, and I don't suppose the place is very pleasant for them now. Anyway, it's best for Gretchen that she not return here."

"What about for you?"

"I don't enter into the calculations at all, my friend. Guess I never really did."

"But surely now that Gretchen feels as she does about Nathan Adams, after years of waiting, he's finally out of the picture. Unless you're not interested anymore?"

"Oh, I'm interested. Hopelessly so. That's what I've finally come to terms with. She's already rebounded, or haven't you noticed the way her gaze follows Gerald about? Well, I guess I've had more opportunities. In short, it seems she's decided to keep her affections within the family. And I'm damned if I'm going to wait around for Gerald to commit suicide. Another drink? No? Me neither. I shall go for a walk," he stumbled as he rose, "and find a rock and vomit behind it, if you'll excuse me. An appropriate end for a fine romance."

Cutter belched with dignity and aimed himself in the direction of the beach. His steps weren't exactly as the crow flies, but Trout judged he'd be all right.

Trout remained in a semireclining position against the tire of the hastily abandoned car. For a moment his thoughts settled on Enid, wondering if she were wondering about him. Then he dismissed her presence from his mind.

He wanted to review what he knew about this case and what he thought others knew. He tried to sort things chronologically, beginning with Nathan Adam's embezzlement and disappearance about a year ago. That was followed by Eve Galatea taking up residence in a Boston apartment building. He allowed himself the parenthetical reassurance that taking all of Halesport County's more bizarre residents, they could not measure up to those in that solitary building.

So Eve Galatea lived in virtual seclusion, but she was not companionless. She kept the inquisitive at bay while she and Nathan concocted the pseudosuicide. But why wait a year? "So he could finish his self-portrait." Trout realized he had spoken aloud and with bitterness.

The time, for whatever reason, was ripe. She drove up here and, after his car was positioned, claimed to find him teetering on the brink and then saw to the delivery of the farewell note covered with his prints.

Then what happened? Gretchen sees him somehow or hears from him, though it seems like a stupid risk on his part. She falls apart at the inquest. So he has a late night rendezvous with his conspirator, discovers that she too is weakening and puts her away for insurance. But Eve Galatea was anything but weak. Queenly, self-possessed, and apparently devoted to Nathan Adams. Why kill her? Maybe it was my influence. Maybe she threatened to tell me all about him.

Well, his fingerprints may not tell me *why* he did it but they tell me *that* he did it. Now I'm stuck with trying to figure out his location. And my possible sources all seem to be slightly demented. Gretchen thinks I should leave well enough—or miserable enough—alone. When I suggest that it is commonly considered to be important to bring murderers to justice she acts as though Eve Galatea never existed. Gerald seems to think I've got a pony tied up waiting to carry him out of town at sundown, but he's going to stick around for High Noon like the cowboy he is. Mrs. Adams wants me to remember my place, which is elsewhere. And Cutter is wallowing in Technicolor memories of a fancy dress party.

Trout closed his eyes and let the images drift by, unbidden and unchecked. Eve Galatea sitting across from him at his desk, very proper, very elegant. The suicide note, according to form, almost arch in its simplicity. The bungling, bumbling lawyer so full of himself. Eve Galatea crumpled on her bed, like something discarded. Launcelot and his ladies posing above the throng. Gretchen lying in shock, murmuring feverishly. That aging caricature of a human being searching for pretexts to invade Eve Galatea's apartment, peering through cracks and praying for disasters. Eve Galatea, swathed in voluminous clothes and shrouded in whispers, stealing to her mailbox. The apartment manager's wife, crisp and starched in her nurse's uniform, bedeviled and besmirched in mufti. Gerald cowering in his mother's drawing room. The uneasy peace achieved between himself and Enid. Mildred Hornsby Adams very proper, very elegant, even in her grief. Alice Collier indignant at, or envious of, his regard for Eve Galatea. Patty Peppermint, or whatever her name was, gum chewing her way to wicked good citizenship, revealing the doctor's pathetic affection for Gretchen. Cutter so single-minded as to devote himself for seven years to the sterile pursuit of his maiden. Agronski methodically digging away until he either unearthed something or reached China. Homer mincing through the case, leaving a trail of bread crumbs. George Cox anointing himself arbiter of the arbitrary common good.

A sudden wave of nausea washed over Trout. Unlike Cutter he didn't attribute it to overindulgence but to enlightenment. He poured himself three fingers of the rum and drained his glass in one quick motion. The alcohol had the desired effect of numbing his body and that part of his brain which triggered his emotions. He ironed his expression to a deadpan and moved purposefully toward the beach.

Though it was quite dark now and the air was thoroughly chilled, the beach was profusely littered with bodies. Apparently all but a few were having too good a time to give up and go home. There was an enormous bonfire ablaze and a few small ones scattered at intervals along the shore. With the onset of night the company had rearranged itself in clusters according to age and interests.

The fire nearest Trout was the hub of the young marrieds who were involved in earnest discussion and harmless flirtations. Another blaze was the focus of teenaged couples who were engaged in a one-on-one exchange of soulful looks and soul kisses. Trout was peripherally embarrassed by their lack of embarrassment. A third fire was encircled by the unattached teenagers who sat gazing into the flames while the ubiquitous girl with overlong straight hair and guitar strummed and sang with little grace and great assurance.

The major conflagration melted the middle-aged, the very old, and the very young together. There was singing here, too. Something for everyone and everyone joined in whether or not the lyrics escaped them or the tune was beyond them. As Trout walked and then stood trying to discern the faces he was treated to renditions of "You Are My Sunshine" and "Yankee Doodle" for the kiddies. Norman Collier was commencing an inspired solo of "Splish Splash" when Enid saw Trout and left the circle.

"Hello?" she said tentatively. "I was a tad worried about you, but then Alice told me you had arrived so I've decided to be offended by your inattentiveness instead."

"Ah, well," he said brightly, "I knew you wouldn't be lacking for male companionship. Norm is always warming the bench and you made a conquest of Dr. Cutter tonight." I don't have time for this conversation, thought Trout.

"You're feeling rather nasty. I was going to suggest that we hold hands and join voices around the fire."

"Later maybe."

"What is it?"

"I have to talk with George."

"Not tonight. You can't mean it. Let him enjoy his party. Please."

"Can't be postponed. Sorry. I don't have any choice."

"Life is full of surprises, as they say," she intoned too blithely. "Here we are after all these years—"

"All these years and three children."

"—and three children and I've only lately learned how insufferably righteous you can be."

"I can't believe that. After all, it's my shortcomings that have brought us so close. What would you offer me in place of understanding?"

With some detachment Trout watched her step back with the force of the blow. She hugged herself as though he had struck her body.

I love her, thought Trout. I wonder why that seems so unimportant. "Do you know where George is?"

She jerked her head from side to side, not in negation as Trout had first assumed, but to shake free from the tears that were forming in her eyes. "By the fire. See him? There." She spoke with a steady voice, giving his position with an inclination of her head. Her hands were still engaged in holding herself together.

"Much obliged. Ah, Cutter, you're ambulatory again, I see."

"But at what price? I've strewn my insides across the beach. At least there was plenty of sand to cover my ignominy." He gave an involuntary shudder and an embarrassed smile.

"Glad to find you sober and upright. Your services are needed."

Cutter stiffened immediately and sighed. "I'm not sure I'm quite that sober. Let me get my bag."

"No instruments necessary. Just your bedside manner. Enid needs comforting," he said, wondering, as though from the vantage point of looking over his own shoulder, just how he would repair the damage he was inflicting.

"You can go straight to hell," Enid said softly to Trout's retreating back.

Trout had caught Cox's eye but remained at a deferential distance while his host completed his conversation. Cox stepped to him, but the welcoming smile and salutations died on his lips as he took in Trout's expression.

"You want to talk," Cox said. He could be criticized for taking himself too seriously, but no one could fault him for not giving the same consideration to others.

"We'll take a stroll down the beach, shall we?" said Trout.

Cox returned his gaze thoughtfully. "We might be interrupted. We'd better use my study."

They retreated to the house. Their progress was checked here and there by roving guests with whom Cox dealt briefly and smoothly. They threaded their way up the back stairs to Cox's second floor study.

As Trout opened the door they heard a scuffling sound. Cox flicked the switch on the wall, and two bodies on the ancient maroon leather sofa flew apart as though the electric current had traveled through them on its route to the overhead light.

Trout noted with mild surprise that one of the bodies was that of his eldest daughter. The other belonged to a vaguely familiar—and singularly unappealing, by Trout's reckoning—teenage male. Trout wondered if the phrase heavy petting was still in current usage. Cox tactfully examined some papers on his desk. Both of the young people were flushed, from embarrassment or exertion. Probably both, Trout decided. They opened their mouths simultaneously and then reconsidered the advisability of speech under Trout's frozen stare. They moved through the door quickly, the boy bolting down the stairs as though Trout's boot had propelled his descent. The girl stood lingering in the hall, her hand holding the door ajar, waiting for her father's first words so she could assess the degree of her disgrace.

"I'm going to tell you what you discovered from the autopsy, George. Stop me if I'm wrong. I'd like that. Because if I'm not wrong you're going to have to turn in that resignation."

There was a small gasp of relief as she pulled the door quietly closed. It'll be okay, she thought. He's got other things on his mind.

CHAPTER 10

Trout emerged alone from the room a half hour later. He paused in the hallway in an attitude that paralleled his daughter's minutes ago. He tried to choose some words to offer to the man barricaded behind the old polished oak desk, but he could find nothing suitable. He closed the door behind him.

He met Sophie Cox on the landing.

"Where's George?" It was more an accusation than a question.

"In the study."

She didn't move and she didn't ask for an explanation. She simply waited. Once again Trout felt the quiet authority of her presence. She hadn't been a disciplinarian in the classroom. She didn't need to be. Pulling his mouth into a banal smile, he excused himself and felt her eyes tunneling into him as he hurried down the stairs.

Despite the steady undercurrent of voices that had permeated the study walls, Trout had expected the party to have thinned out considerably by now. In his single-mindedness he was unprepared to deal with anyone except the one person he sought. Yet, at least indoors, the numbers seemed to have swelled in his brief absence.

He was hailed, hugged, buffeted, and bussed from all sides as he tried vainly to escape from the house.

He was overwhelmed by the feeling that the world was populated by his friends, neighbors, and relatives and there was no comfort in the sensation. The amiable figures around him were beginning to assume nightmarish proportions when he was tackled by his Aunt Agatha, who took him to task for his failure to pay court earlier in the evening. Murmuring something—he wondered what he had said, as he could recall only the picture of her carefully plucked and painted eyebrows shooting up to meet her hairline—he charged through the door, leaving a trail of jostled elbows and bruised insteps behind him.

Once outside, he examined what he could think of as nothing other than a lapse of sanity. He had been so driven to complete this wretched business that any impediment, even in the nature of a hearty handshake, seemed part of a conspiracy to frustrate him. He wondered if he had experienced claustrophobia, paranoia, or fanaticism or if those were really all synonymous.

A measure of calm pervaded him, but he still regarded the ordeal of sifting through all these bodies with distaste. He consoled himself with a cigarette. As he bent to extinguish the stub in the sand, he saw, rather than heard, the approach of two expensive and inappropriate leather half boots.

In what Trout took to be an egalitarian gesture, Gerald Adams lowered himself onto the sand beside him. Glancing pointedly at Trout's burrowing hand, Gerald asked, "Lost a contact lens?"

It was a poor attempt at humor but it was the only one Trout had ever heard him make and, ironically enough, it saddened Trout keenly.

"I've found all the pieces," Trout said woodenly.

Gerald's brow furrowed in his effort to penetrate this obviously loaded statement.

"You gave me too much credit before. I didn't understand at all."

"And now you do?"

"Now I do.

Gerald nodded slowly, rhythmically.

"What happens now?"

"I have to arrest you for murder."

"I thought—I guess I hoped—you'd let it go."

"For money?"

"No." Gerald's voice was stretched taut now. "I never thought of money. Is that what you want?"

"No." Trout met his eyes for the first time. "Why did you think I'd let you go?"

"A lot of reasons, I suppose. My mother seems the most obvious one. It will very possibly kill her." There was no plea in his voice.

"Yes, I see that," Trout said just as calmly and as clinically.

"And poor Gretchen. She's not strong enough yet. A trial and all the ugly publicity," Gerald shrugged, "she'd never survive. Not intact, anyway."

"I don't suppose so."

"And then I didn't intend to do it."

"I know."

"She—it—taunted me. I didn't go there with a gun." He was deathly quiet for a moment. "You know, she tried—made a game of trying—to seduce me that night. I was sick, utterly sick. Of myself. Of everything. She counted on that. That's when she gave me the gun. With instructions on how to use it. She recommended inserting the nozzle in my mouth.

"I did it. Put it in my mouth, I mean. You know I can still taste that gun? But she laughed too soon, and I killed her. And you blame me?"

"No. I envy you."

"But you'll arrest me all the same."

"Yes."

"Why?"

"It's my job."

"I'm sorry that's the way you see it."

"So am I, but that's the way I see it. It won't be as stiff as you think. Even the county prosecutor will be on your side. One way or another, you'll get off."

"It's not prison I'm afraid of, though I don't relish the idea. It's everybody knowing."

"Yeah. I know."

"That's the whole trouble isn't it?" They smiled weakly at each other. "Well, if you don't mind telling me, how did you unravel our sordid little mystery?"

"Cutter was in his cups, reminiscing about the fancy dress ball. Everything, as they say, fell into place."

"I see. So if it weren't for unrequited love and/or demon rum, I'd be free—of all this?"

"More than likely. It's not something that would have occurred to me on my own. And if George Cox had his way, all the good folk of Halesport County would be protected from this unseemly knowledge."

"Not a bad idea, that."

"One thing still bothers me, Gerald—how did she get Nathan's car up to the overlook? She drove up from Boston in a rental car, so who brought the Audi into the area? I can't imagine her entrusting that job to anyone. Not to mention the considerable risk of the Audi being recognized."

"She gloated about that. The day of the disappearance she hid it in the abandoned cannery on the gravel turnoff just beyond the overlook. The car never left Fells Harbor."

"Another piece of egg on my chin."

"I don't think you can blame yourself much for that oversight. The FBI never searched for the Audi in this vicinity either. I mean, it's reasonable to look for a getaway car someplace away from the site of departure."

"That night did she—did she say anything about me?"

"No," said Gerald too promptly. "No. Nothing at all."

Playing Launcelot again, thought Trout, sensitive to the chivalry of the denial. Gerald was right: better not to know. "I've staggered through this case like a newborn calf—just our bad luck I had to stumble on the truth," he apologized. "I'm going to corner Agronski now. He'll take you back to . . . town. Do I need to concern myself with your immediate plans?"

"I'm not running. It would serve no purpose. I'd like to take my leave of George and Sophie. No? Oh, I see. They've been apprised of my situation. Well, we don't want to make things awkward for anyone, do we?" There was only the merest tinge of belligerence in his voice. "Then I shall locate my mother, with your permission, and give her some explanation for my departure. I'd rather she not be informed of all this until morning."

"I'll take you to the house myself tomorrow. You can tell her then."

"Can you do that? Thank you. I'll have to speak with Gretchen. That will be more difficult. She'll know, of course, that I've been arrested, but I think that for Mother's sake she'll be able to put up a front for this one night."

"Okay. When you're finished just come back here. Agronski will be waiting."

Trout knew it would be easier for Gerald if he were to take him in, but he couldn't bring himself to do that.

Trout shuffled down to the circle of young marrieds. Agronski and his wife were there, each balancing a dozing child on a shoulder. Agronski was holding forth on the subject of civil disobedience when he noticed Trout standing some yards off. He rose smoothly without disturbing the sleep of his young son and covered the distance between them.

"Sir?" he said.

Trout wondered if the sand had muffled the sound of his heels clicking together.

"I want you to go over to that sandy stretch by those fir trees there and wait for Gerald Adams. Then drive him in, and book him on suspicion of murder. Tell Homer to bunk in the other cell for the night and that he should make the prisoner as comfortable as possible. I don't want Homer's mouth set loose

on this town until I've had a chance to talk to him, and I won't
get around to that until morning. Any questions?"

This last was rather cruel on Trout's part, as he knew that
Agronski had dozens and was struggling to keep his mouth shut
and follow orders like a good soldier.

"One, sir. Do I book him for the murder of Eve Galatea?"

Trout started to say something, thought better of it, then
instructed, "For the murder of Nathan Adams."

Trout had to acknowledge a grudging admiration for
Agronski. He hadn't even blinked in response to Trout's
announcement—just deposited the child on a blanket on the
sand and then on to execute his duty.

"I've been looking all over for you," Cutter broke into his
thoughts. "Your wife asked me to tell you she had gone home
with your daughters."

"Thanks."

"If you don't mind my saying so, I think you're crazy."

"I don't mind. In fact, I'm considering using temporary
insanity as my plea for her mercy. You can be my expert
witness."

"You don't seem to appreciate what you have."

"Are you her advocate now? I don't need to be told her
virtues."

"Sorry. I'm sure you don't. I told you my tale of woe. Care
to reciprocate?"

"Why not? You'll hear all about it tomorrow, anyway. As a
matter of fact, you probably should know tonight so you can
hold yourself in readiness. You'll be needed at the Hornsby
House in the morning."

"Why? What's happened?"

"We've arrested Gerald Adams."

"Gerald? Whatever for?"

"Murder."

"But that's preposterous. He'd no motive for killing the
Galatea woman."

"He had a strong motive for killing his brother."

"Have you turned up Nathan's body?"

"Under the circumstances, that qualifies as a trick question."

"What are you talking about?"

"Eve Galatea and Nathan Adams were one and the same."

"You really are crazy."

"Gerald's admitted it. Not that it can't be proved. I would have known this days ago if our host had seen fit to reveal his findings from the autopsy. He found evidence of plastic surgery and a transsexual operation. In the tradition of the landed gentry protecting its serfs, he chose to keep this rather noisome bit of information to himself and protect us all from the breath of scandal.

"In his defense I have to say that he was disturbed enough about his decision to leave town and seek the counsel of some of his old cronies and that he concluded—incorrectly, as we know—that it was not relevant to determining who killed her—him."

"Are you sure of all this?" Cutter couldn't mask his incredulity.

"There's an abundance of supporting evidence. Eve Galatea took an apartment in Boston around the time of Nathan's disappearance. She was seldom there in the first months— believed to be traveling. In fact, undergoing various surgical procedures. When she did settle in she was rarely seen, and then only under mounds of clothing. It took some time before the butterfly was able to emerge from her chrysalis. Even after she shed her cocoon, she spoke seldom and only in whispers. That must have been the most difficult part—training herself to speak with the voice of a woman.

"Then she set about establishing her identity, in case we checked on her as a witness to the suicide. That was achieved in part with the aid of a doltish lawyer.

"Now that we know what name to look for, I'm sure we'll find the rest of the embezzled money in a European account.

"Anyway, having a safe identity, it was time to get rid of Nathan Adams. Hence the sham suicide."

"But why come back here to do it? Why take the risk?"

"What risk? You saw her at the inquest, and you didn't recognize her. Mildred Hornsby Adams was there and didn't even recognize her own son.

"Maybe in part she came back because if Nathan Adams' death were accepted here, it wouldn't be questioned anywhere else. Maybe. I think she came back because she couldn't resist it. She wanted to defy anyone to recognize her. But mostly she wanted to watch. Watch her mother, her brother, Gretchen. Watch them mourn Nathan Adams."

"But Gretchen did recognize her. On the stand." Cutter shuddered.

"Yes. That was unexpected. She changed her plans, decided to stay on and see what might develop. I don't think she was very worried even then though. Gretchen could be counted on for her unswerving loyalty. And even if Gretchen wanted to destroy Eve Galatea, she wouldn't do it at the risk of destroying Mildred Adams.

"What Eve Galatea hadn't foreseen was that in a moment of weakness following her own suicide attempt Gretchen would confide in Gerald."

"But Gerald wouldn't have believed such a story coming from Gretchen. We all felt she was unbalanced."

"Yes, but he also knew his brother Nathan. Gerald never quite believed in the death by drowning story. So, even if he wasn't convinced by Gretchen, he was at least determined to lay his doubts to rest.

"So that night, after you and Mrs. Adams had gone to bed, Gretchen told Gerald. Mrs. Adams heard him close his door before she fell asleep, but he wasn't behind it. He was leaving for the cottage where Eve Galatea was staying.

"They played a rather loathsome scene there. She denied everything at first, I suppose. Then made sexual advances toward Gerald, admitting everything, sparing Gerald no detail. His opinion of himself has never been consistently high, and it didn't take much skill on her part to pile her shame atop his and bury him under a mass of self-disgust. She offered him her pistol and better luck in the next world. I suppose the most astonishing thing about this whole case is that Gerald didn't kill himself. Not even after he shot her.

"We never got the chance to find out how she intended to explain Gerald's corpse away. Something ingenious, no doubt.

"Anyway, next day we dusted the cottage for prints and came up with two clear sets. I made the mistake of assuming since they were identical and found on her belongings that they were necessarily hers. Agronski, a good and thorough fellow, followed up on the prints. They belonged to Nathan Adams. So we concluded that Nathan was alive and had killed Eve, who had been his conspirator. I never had her prints checked." Trout shook his head in disbelief at his own words. "Of course, when she gave evidence about Nathan's jump, it wasn't procedure to print her. She was investigated and came up smelling like an orchid. And after she was murdered—well, when Agronski turned up Nathan's prints, it seemed like I had all the information I needed, except Nathan's location."

"His prints on the car and the suicide letter," Cutter mused, "a good touch. And as long as the Galatea identity was never prosecuted for a crime, she had nothing to fear."

"That's about it." Trout paused and then his fury found its focus. "I think I could have understood if Nathan Adams had wanted to be a woman and because of that used his position to embezzle the money needed for the operations and to establish a new identity." Trout realized with a start that he had confused his pronouns. When he continued, the bitter edge to his voice cut through the darkness, exposing his own wound. "I could have understood if she hadn't any choice. But her body was a tool to get the money. The sex change was just the ultimate manipulation."

They were both quiet for a time, then Cutter said, "Gerald doesn't deserve this. She—he—had to be killed. It wasn't murder, it was a public service."

"I do my job."

Struggling between anger and compassion, Cutter stared at him. Compassion for the man next to him and perhaps a professional sense of duty tipped the scales. "Yes. Of course."

"It won't be a charge of first degree," Trout said in his own defense. "And you can count on his having the best lawyer and the sympathy of everyone. He'll get off pretty lightly."

"But Gretchen and Mrs. Adams?"

"That's where you come in."

"What can I do?"

"Be there. You said Mrs. Adams is talking of selling the Hornsby house. Convince her to give up their New York apartment instead. She'll want to be here through the trial, anyway. Once she's gotten through that, she'll discover how many friends she has here. In New York—anyplace else for that matter—she and Gretchen would be objects of morbid curiosity. The people won't let that happen here. And Gretchen would have you."

"That's all over for me now."

"If you say so."

"Well, there's something in what you say. They probably would be better off here. I'll see what I can do."

They shook hands formally and Trout walked in the direction of his car.

He was contemplating a long ride in the Alfa with no particular destination when a panting Agronski approached from his rear, calling "Sir!" over and over.

Trout was trying to appear not to hear the thunder beating up the path behind him. He wasn't in the mood to pat the deputy's head or discuss with boy scout seriousness some aspect of the case that was troubling him.

"Yes?" he said, turning sharply as he reached the car and there was no way to add to the distance between them. "What is it?"

"Gerald Adams is in his cell. Everything satisfactory on that count. Homer's a bit bewildered, though."

"Fine," said Trout in dismissal.

Agronski hesitated, then said "Sir?" again.

"Well?" Trout's lips moved, but his teeth were firmly clenched.

"I've been thinking over your suggestion, sir, and I discussed it with my wife. She agreed that the time is right for that sort of step in our lives. We spoke with a few people, just to see if the idea would strike anyone as—outrageous. You know. The feedback was positive, I'm pleased to say, so I will be running for sheriff in the coming election. I wanted you to know prior to any official announcement, of course, and I wanted to thank you for what you've taught me and for, well, encouraging me."

Trout's reaction shifted from befuddled irritation to amazement. He stood leaning against the open car door, staring past Agronski. He ran his tongue over the inside of his mouth and found he was able to move his jaw again.

Trout got into the Alfa, pulled the door shut, turned on the ignition and rolled down the window. He thought he was smiling at Agronski as he said, "Well, why not?"